CHIPPED

LUX THORN

THE WHUMPY PRINTING PRESS

Cover Illustration by Hen Towers

Cover Design by Nicole Alessi

Also By the Author

CONTENTS

CONTENT WARNINGS

This story contains the following content:

- Heavy violence, including knives, guns, blood, torture, and electrocution

- Mind control

- Institutionalized slavery

- Toxic relationship

- Major character death

If this book isn't for you, no worries! But if it is, we hope you enjoy this story about a torturer and his rebel...

1

— · —

Ryland hated when prisoners pissed themselves.

Blood he could handle. Blood was just part of the job. If he wanted to get information out of a prisoner, chances were someone was going to have to bleed for that information, and it wasn't going to be him. But the acrid smell of urine was enough to make him regret the hasty muffin he had grabbed on his way to work. He should have stuck with his usual breakfast of black coffee.

The prisoner quivered against the steel cuffs that bound his wrists and ankles to the chair. Wetness spread across his pants. Pungent liquid dripped down onto the smooth gray concrete of the floor to dilute the small pool of blood there. The man's eyes remained locked on the bloody knife in Ryland's hand.

Funny – he'd handled electricity just fine. Better than fine – Ryland had brought in one of the techs to make sure the current was strong enough, he'd resisted so well. But as soon as Ryland had started cutting, the man had fallen apart like a wet tissue. Ryland could usually tell which methods would break any given prisoner the fastest. Call it a sixth sense. It wounded his pride when he was wrong.

Ryland ripped off the remaining electrodes, taking no notice of the prisoner's flinch each time the sticky adhesive tore away from his skin. He wouldn't be needing those anymore. The knife in his hand was all he needed.

He brought it close to the trembling man's face, the tip nearly brushing his cheek. The man pulled back as far as he could, his eyes round, his cuffs rattling against the chair as he trembled.

"All I need," he said, "is the key to the cipher you created for the resistance."

His eyes still locked on the knife, the man shook his head weakly. "I didn't create that cipher." His voice was thin, desperate, trembling with the obvious lie. "It wasn't me. I told you."

Ryland lowered the knife until the tip was pointing at the floor directly in front of the chair. At the scrap of what had been the top half of the man's pinky finger, severed at the highest knuckle.

The man followed his gaze. The rattling increased.

One more finger ought to do it. Ryland sighed to himself. The thought of another gush of blood, of another round of piercing screams that had almost shattered his eardrum the first time, made him want to put the knife down and adjourn for a nap in his office – and it wasn't even lunchtime yet. At least the man didn't have any more piss in him.

He stared down at the bit of severed flesh. His stomach churned. Wasn't a single mutilation enough for one day?

He clenched his teeth. Not this again. This reticence, this … *weakness.* None of this ever used to bother him – not the blood, not the screams, not whatever mangled mess he had to make of a prisoner before they gave up what he wanted. Not until he had started imagining Coop's face superimposed on the face of every prisoner in his interrogation room. Coop's blood. Coop's screams. Coop's severed finger on the floor.

Ryland dropped the knife at his feet. It landed with a clatter on the concrete.

"You've already lost one finger today," he said. "It seems excessive to take any more. Your wife, now … she's still got a full set of ten. For now. She usually goes to the Sub Shack for lunch, right? If she follows her usual schedule, she should be getting there about, oh…" He made a show of checking his watch. "Half an hour from now." He laced his hands behind his back and leaned back casually, resting his weight on his back foot. "I'm willing to wait. How about you?"

Ryland's intuition had been wrong about this prisoner before. But not this time. With a strangled sob, the man hung his head. "Don't … don't touch her." His voice was a thready whisper.

"I'm waiting," said Ryland.

When he looked up at Ryland, his eyes were dead. "You'll need to write this down."

***

On his way out for an early lunch, Ryland caught the sound of tuneless whistling behind him.

He only knew one person that bad at carrying a tune.

Ryland picked up his pace. The whistling stopped. "Interrogator Eskell!" a jolly voice called. "Just the man I was hoping to see."

Ryland briefly considered pretending he hadn't heard. Then turned to face his boss, Elmer Norby, a diminutive man with a baby face and lips perpetually puckered from kissing his own bosses' asses. Norby flashed him a smile. "How goes it with the Johnson interrogation?"

"Just finished with him. You'll have the cipher – as well as a few names he knew – this afternoon. After I celebrate with a long lunch." Ryland held Norby's gaze, silently daring the man to heap another urgent assignment on him immediately after this victory.

Norby's eyes fell to Ryland's cuff. He wrinkled his nose. "You might want to get yourself cleaned up first."

Ryland followed Norby's gaze. There was a single speck of blood on his cuff. Somehow, despite supervising a building full of interrogators, Norby still hadn't gotten the idea that interrogation was a bloody job. Probably because he got to sit behind his desk all day and keep his hands clean.

There was a time he used to meticulously check himself for blood before he left the building. Coop had always hated it when he showed up with traces of his work still on him. It reminded Coop of all manner of things he preferred not to think about.

"It was a hard interrogation," was all he said now.

"You've been going above and beyond lately." Norby gave him a hearty pat on the shoulder. Ryland held still and endured it. "That's exactly why I wanted to talk to you. I've got something that's about to make your life a lot easier."

Ryland, adept at reading prisoners, caught the not-so-subtle signs of strain in his boss's too-wide smile. He looked like someone trying to convince a kid that a cup of foul-tasting medicine was going to taste good.

"I'm sure you've found yourself wishing for an extra pair of hands from time to time," Norby continued, his voice painfully bright. "Someone to fill out your paperwork for you, or hold your ... tools ... in the interrogation room ... " He made the grimace he always did when he was forced to talk, however obliquely, about what actually happened during interrogations.

Ryland sighed. "Not another intern. The last one fainted at the sight of blood."

"You won't have that problem with this one!" Norby promised. "He's not an intern. He's something better. Obedient, highly trainable, and he'll never ask for a raise." He chuckled too hard at his own joke.

Ryland tried to parse this. When he worked it out, he stared. "Tell me you're not considering bringing a *chipped worker* into a secure facility."

A wince cracked Norby's smile. "It's no secret how you feel about chipped workers – "

"I'm not the only one. They're a security risk – that's been established. The technology isn't infallible." Chipped workers were the government's answer to a surfeit of rebels and a shortage of workers. The chip, inserted just behind the ear, promised to make a former rebel docile and obedient, with little memory of their past and no desire to rebel. By all accounts, they made highly useful factory workers, and chip failures were rare. But rare didn't mean nonexistent, and giving a potential time bomb free run of a factory was a far cry from setting one loose *here.*

Besides ... privately, Ryland found the idea grotesque. The fact that the technology existed to strip someone's past from them, their will, their *humanity*, was something he preferred not to think about.

"I took a careful look at the data before I agreed to this," Norby assured him. "The chips are a lot hardier than they used to be. Left alone, they'll keep working for a hundred years – longer than any chipped worker's lifetime. And there's no physically damaging the chip, short of shooting the worker in the head or shorting it out with enough electricity to stop their heart –

and both of those would solve any problems before they started, wouldn't they?" He gave another too-loud chuckle.

"What about the effects on higher cognition?" Ryland asked. "There's a reason chipped workers are normally assigned to menial jobs. My work requires more than pulling a lever for ten hours a day."

"There have been major advances in the technology. The chips are not only more resilient, they have less of an effect on essential brain functions. That's why the technology division wants to do a trial run expanding the uses of chipped workers – and you're one of the first lucky beneficiaries." Norby's smile was back, even more strained around the edges now.

"I appreciate the offer," Ryland lied through his teeth, "but I'm sure someone else would appreciate it more. Assign this worker to someone else." Anyone else.

"You're considered the best equipped for this trial, because of your ... ability to respond quickly and decisively should the need arise." There came that grimace again.

"You mean I have a reputation for brutality," said Ryland. "Just in case I'm right and this worker is a security breach waiting to happen. I'd rather not take the risk in the first place."

"Consider this an additional job responsibility," said Norby, his smile dying away. "One that comes with some added benefits. I know you could use that extra pair of hands."

"You pay me to interrogate prisoners," said Ryland. "Not to be a test subject for the technology division. Tell me, how much extra funding did your bosses promise you for next year in exchange for signing us up as guinea pigs?"

Norby's smile faded. His cheeks went pink. "Well, it's too late to send him back now, so you may as well make the best – "

"Send him *back*? He's already here?"

"The technology division delivered him this morning," said Norby. "He's waiting in your office."

With a muttered curse, Ryland turned his back on his boss – he could worry about the ramifications of his rudeness later – and hurried down the hall toward his office.

A rebel with a head full of questionable technology. In *his* office, alone with a computer full of secure files. And he had been there *how* long?

But when he threw open the door to his office, there were two men waiting for him, not one. The first, wearing the blue uniform of the technology division, was sitting in Ryland's chair. He looked up with a frown. "It's about time. I've been waiting here since – "

He probably said more. Ryland didn't hear it.

He stared at the man standing in the center of the room, and forgot how to breathe.

The standing man was wearing a darker blue than the other, his shirt and pants rough and plain. His hair was shorn nearly down to the scalp. He stood with his arms pressed tightly to his sides, staring at a point just below his eye level. His face was expressionless, his eyes blank and glassy.

But Ryland remembered when those shorn curls had been long enough to hang into his eyes. He remembered that face creased with laughter, and blotchy with fury as he threw one of Ryland's blood-flecked shirts at his head. He remembered the softness of those lips on his, and those glassy eyes bright with adoration.

Coop, he mouthed, barely stopping himself from saying the name aloud.

Cooper Byrd. The rebel he had fallen in love with, even though he had known better. The rebel who had haunted Ryland since his arrest. Ever since Ryland had failed to save him – because trying to save him would have meant risking his own life.

2

The last time Ryland had seen Coop, they hadn't been speaking. Ryland hadn't looked at Coop as he had pulled his shirt back on, their planned liaison cut short because of yet another argument. When he had glanced up at Coop, Coop had been sitting on the edge of the narrow bed in the one-room apartment. Ryland could still picture his face as it had been that night, tight with anger, staring into Ryland's eyes as if daring Ryland to look away again.

He hadn't said a word – they were all done with words for that night, the familiar tense silence all that was left between them. But their arguments still echoed off the thin walls.

"You're never going to leave, are you?"

"I got us both new identities – good ones. A bank account that can't be tracked. I bought us a cabin, for god's sake, in a little town in the woods where no one will look for us." Ryland could still hear the defensiveness in his voice, could still feel the tightness in his throat. *"Is that not enough commitment for you? What more do you want?"*

"How about for you to actually do it?"

"It's not the right time."

Another image, burned into Ryland's brain: Coop's hair flying into his eyes as he shook his head. *"You've been saying that for months. It's never going to be the right time, is it? I don't think you want to give it up – the good job, the nice house, the secret boyfriend on the side. You don't care that you're paying for all that with the blood of my friends."*

"You mean your friends who are willing to let the world burn so long as it means people like me burn first? I thought we were done with that argument. I'm willing to give up everything for you. Isn't that enough?"

"Are you willing? Because you're sure not showing it."

Ryland had hurried out of the apartment with his shirt still half-buttoned, unable to face Coop's accusing gaze one second longer. In this neighborhood, there were no cameras – even an obvious rebel around here would have had to worry more about a stolen wallet than an arrest. Even the streetlights were broken. The anonymity was the reason they had chosen this place to rent for their illicit nights together. Still, Ryland had looked up and down the street as he turned away, looking for signs of Coop's people watching, looking for his own. Unsure which would be worse for both of them.

He had told himself not to look over his shoulder, but he had done it anyway. Coop had been there at the window, lips curled in disgust, judging Ryland's twitchiness about surveillance. As if he wasn't just as worried about being discovered with Ryland as Ryland was about being discovered with him. As if he wasn't ashamed of sharing a bed for two stolen nights a week with a man who wore an interrogator's uniform during the day.

Coop hadn't shown up for their next planned meeting. Ryland had assumed he was still angry. Until a fit of what he had thought was irrational fear had made him check the database at work, and he had seen Coop's name staring out at him from the screen like an accusation.

How many times since then had Ryland longed for one last look at Coop, one more glimpse of him to erase the terrible memory of those eyes full of bitter condemnation? Now, as the man who used to be Coop stared through him with empty eyes, Ryland regretted every time he had made that wish.

The tech sitting in Ryland's chair checked his watch. "There some kind of problem? Or will you go ahead and sign off that he's been delivered? The agreement says you're responsible for him during the standard workday. The facility is obligated to provide storage at night, and basic care on weekends and holidays. If he dies, one of us will have to certify that it was natural causes, or there'll be a fine. Basic stuff." He held out a screen to Ryland. "I've got other places to be today, you know. I didn't expect to be here so long."

Ryland gave the screen a brief, distracted glance. Then his eyes were pulled back to the man with Coop's face, as if magnetized. "What's his name?" As if there was any question. As if he could possibly be mistaken.

The tech frowned. "The worker's? How the hell should I know? He probably doesn't even remember it. Call him whatever you like – he'll learn to answer to it." The man stood, holding out the screen more insistently.

"I'm Ryland," Ryland said to Coop's blank face. "Ryland Eskell." He searched those glassy eyes, and saw no hint of recognition.

"Hello," Coop said in a voice as flat as his face. "It's a pleasure to meet you." He held out his hand.

Coop had loathed the custom of shaking hands – *What's polite about being socially obligated to touch the hand the other guy probably scratched his ass with five minutes ago?* Ryland stared at the outstretched hand, and couldn't bring himself to take it. Would Coop's skin still feel the same – silky soft, like the luxurious sheets Ryland couldn't afford even on his salary?

The tech huffed. "There's no point in talking to them. Tell him what you want him to do, he'll do it. Better tell him to eat and sleep and piss too, or he'll work for three days straight before passing out in his own mess. But don't expect decent conversation." He pressed the screen into Ryland's hand. "Now, are we finished here, or ... "

Ryland, who had come in here ready to throw the chipped worker out on his ear, used his finger to sign without a word.

With a mutter under his breath that sounded like, *It's about time*, the tech hurried out the door and closed it behind him. And then it was just Ryland and Coop. Or Ryland and the thing that wasn't quite Coop. The thing that wasn't quite human.

Coop finally lowered his hand. He stood perfectly still, until Ryland had to squint to make sure he was breathing.

Ryland walked past him to his desk. He froze momentarily as his arm brushed Coop's. A bolt of electricity shot through him – sense-memory and repulsion wrapped into one. Coop didn't react.

Ryland slid into his chair. With a few quick keystrokes, he disabled the surveillance in his office. Then, still sitting, he swiveled to face Coop.

Coop was still facing the other way, staring at the closed door. "Hey," Ryland said softly. "Hey, look at me."

Instantly, Coop turned to face him, his glassy eyes locking on Ryland's face. A shiver crawled up Ryland's spine.

"Cooper," Ryland said. "Cooper Byrd."

A tiny crease between Coop's eyebrows marred the smooth expressionlessness of his face. "I'm sorry. I don't know what you mean."

"That's your name. You really don't remember?" How could a person forget an entire life? How could he forget his name, his dislike of handshakes, his loathing for the building he stood inside now? How could he forget the man who had shared his bed for two long years?

But the technology division had had almost a decade to perfect the chips. Tens of thousands of test subjects, from the early failures to the first successes to the man who stood in front of Ryland now.

It had never mattered to Ryland until it was Coop.

Even though Ryland knew better, he tried again anyway. "Coop." He whispered it the way he might once have in bed.

"Is that what you'd like to call me?" Coop's voice, soft and even, was the worst thing Ryland had ever heard.

Ryland stared into those eyes, and saw nothing. The man in front of him might as well have been a doll with a painted face. No – not a doll. A corpse. He looked dead, and maybe he was. Maybe the man Ryland had known was gone, killed by the thing sitting in his brain.

Maybe that was a kinder fate than if Coop had been trapped in there, lost in his own mind, screaming and unable to be heard.

Ryland shook away another shiver. He forced his eyes away.

Yes – Coop was dead. Better to think of it that way. The man in front of him wore his face and spoke with his voice, but that was all. Now if only Ryland could send him back, so he would only have to worry about his own memories haunting him. He already regretted signing, but of course, by now the tech was long gone.

His stomach growled, reminding him that he still hadn't had that lunch. His desire to go out and celebrate had fled. He would grab something quick from the cafeteria, and then he would get back to work. Since it was too late to send Coop – to send the *chipped worker* – back, he would do what Norby wanted, and use him as an extra pair of hands until he was numb to the sight of him.

He stood. "I'm getting lunch," he said, although he had a feeling he could have left his office without a word and the other man would not have felt a single shred of curiosity about where he had gone. "Don't touch anything while I'm gone." Belatedly, he remembered the tech's words. Coop – the chipped worker – wouldn't feed himself, which meant it was presumably Ryland's job to feed him. "You want anything?"

The voice that answered was just as soft as before, but this time, it held an unmistakable hint of mischief. "A handsome model in my bed and enough money that I never have to work again," he said, as Ryland froze, wide-eyed. "But if you're asking about *lunch*, I'd settle for ham and cheese."

It was the same joke he always used to make. Ryland used to tease him about it – *It's not funny the hundredth time, you know.* That was before he had known that someday he would give anything to hear it one more time.

It took Ryland a few seconds to find his voice. "What did you say?"

"I said I'd like ham and cheese, if you wouldn't mind," Coop said in his too-flat voice. The hint of mischief was gone.

"No. Before that. What did you say?"

But Coop only stared at him in confusion. His eyes were just as dead as they had been a moment ago.

The man had never made Coop's old joke, had he? Because he wasn't Coop.

It was just the same old ghost in Ryland's head, haunting him again.

Still, as he left, he looked over his shoulder. He could have sworn he saw Coop's eyes following him as he walked away.

3

—·—

The chipped worker couldn't still be Coop on the inside. His lack of expression as they walked into the interrogation room was the proof. Coop's face was blank, his stride steady, as he took in the stark concrete floor and the gleaming metal cabinets concealing an impressive array of tools. He didn't even react as his eyes fell on the prisoner cuffed to the metal chair at the center of the room.

This was her first interrogation. Her face still held more defiance than fear, which wasn't the case for most prisoners who had sat in one of these chairs for more than a couple of hours. Her only bruises were from her arrest – the note in her file explained that she had resisted. Ryland looked away from Coop long enough to take in her clenched fists, her rigid back, the snarl of fury on her face. All signs of a prisoner who thought raw anger would be enough to get them through what was coming.

Ordinarily, that sight would have cheered Ryland – more often than not, it meant an easy interrogation. But now it set his teeth on edge. He knew he could anticipate being cursed at and spat on before the prisoner's curses devolved into screams. And speaking of screams, there were likely to be plenty of those too. The angriest prisoners tended to be the loudest.

He looked over his shoulder at the door, contemplating simply walking back out of the room. Maybe he could knock off early for once. Between his victory this morning and the sixty-hour weeks he'd been working lately, he had earned it.

But that meant admitting defeat.

A small intake of breath from the prisoner made him realize he had stopped watching her. He was staring at Coop again, at that corpselike face. He turned back to the prisoner in time to see her anger shift to shock, then a sick horror. Not an uncommon reaction for prisoners who realized what was about to happen to them, but she wasn't looking at Ryland anymore.

She was looking at Coop.

"Cooper," she whispered.

So she had known him, then. Probably worked with him in the resistance. Absolutely fucking fantastic. Her horrified whisper grated on him as much as he imagined her screams would later. Speaking of sounds, why was the ventilation system so *loud* today? And the room was just slightly too hot, sending a prickly itch up his torso. Had someone messed with the temperature controls?

"Cooper," the prisoner repeated, louder this time. Her voice wasn't any less irritating at a normal volume. "Can you hear me?"

"He's not going to answer," Ryland said, his voice short. "He's – "

"Chipped," the prisoner finished for him. "I know that look. I know what it means." He expected a return to her snarling fury, a torrent of curses – all the old tired insults he had heard before. Instead, she lowered her head. "I'm sorry, Cooper. I wondered what had happened when you disappeared. I hoped it wasn't this."

Ryland snapped his fingers in front of her face. She flinched back.

"You're not here to talk to him," he reminded her. "You're here to talk to me." He shifted so he was standing between her and Coop. Then he stared down at her, crossing his arms, and willed himself not to look over his shoulder at Coop's unnatural stillness.

"Here's the situation," he said. "Everything you've heard about what happens in this building is considerably better than the reality. And I happen to be having a very bad day, so I'm not inclined to go easy on you."

She opened her mouth. He kept going before she could speak. Whatever she was going to say, it would only set his nerves jangling even more. How could her voice possibly be so annoying? And that *face*. Those beady little eyes, like a pig.

And what was going on with the temperature in here, anyway? The room felt even hotter now than it had a moment ago. A thin sheen of sweat coated his forehead.

"You were arrested breaking into a secure facility," he continued, "so don't try to deny anything. We have the video footage."

She tilted her head to the side. What was she ... oh, of course. She was still trying to look at Coop. He shifted again to block her view.

"Here's what I need from you," he said. "The names of all your co-conspirators – the three who escaped when we arrested you, plus anyone who helped you plan that little escapade of yours. If you give me everything – and I mean everything – you may just earn yourself a clean death instead of ending up like *him*."

Finally, he stepped aside, giving her a view of Coop once more. He itched to look over his shoulder himself, but didn't.

She swallowed at the sight of him. "Cooper," she said again. "Come on, Cooper. You've got to be in there somewhere."

"Do you need something to help you focus on me and not him? Very well – I can manage that." Ryland stalked across the room and threw open one of the cabinets. The metal door hit the wall with a clang. "Pain has a way of focusing a person's attention, I've found."

He pulled out a pair of gleaming steel pliers, freshly disinfected. "We'll start with your fingernails," he said. "I'll give you a little break after each one. That will give you ten chances to start feeling more cooperative."

A shiver ran through the prisoner. She tucked her fingers protectively under her palms. "You're pathetic, you know that?" Her voice shook.

"Not the response I would have chosen." Ryland advanced on her, holding the pliers in one hand.

"You're not even going to try to talk to me first? You're just going straight to ripping out fingernails?" Her voice dripped with contempt, even as her eyes shone with fear. "Is brutality really the only tool you have?"

Coop used to ask him how he could live with himself. There had been times he would flinch away from Ryland's touch, saying he couldn't stand the feeling of those hands on his skin, knowing what they had done only hours before. Of course, when they were in bed, his conscience had never stopped him from begging for more.

Ryland's hand tightened around the pliers. He held them up in front of the prisoner's face, snapping them shut just to watch her flinch. That wasn't like him – he didn't enjoy a prisoner's fear unless he thought it meant the prisoner was that much closer to breaking. But now he took satisfaction in the way she drew back from him – and, most of all, in her silence.

"I've got plenty of tools in my toolbox," he informed her. "You'll see a lot of them, unless you start cooperating soon. As for my methods, you wouldn't have been assigned to me if my boss thought simple persuasion would be enough to get through to you. I've got a reputation in this building. Most of those stories you heard? They were about *me*." He flashed her a joyless smile.

What's wrong with me? Coop had asked one night as they lay in bed, turning his head away from Ryland. *I'm sick in the head. I've got to be. This – what we're doing – it's sick.*

"Hold her hand in place," Ryland snapped to Coop. "We'll start with the left. Straighten her fingers for me."

Cooper showed no hesitation as he walked over and grabbed her hand. She looked up at Coop, then quickly away, her eyes wet. "You don't have to do this," she said to him. "You can fight it."

"He doesn't know who you are," Ryland reminded her.

This was when he would normally give the prisoner one more chance to cooperate before things got messy. But what was the point? She wasn't going to give him anything yet. He knew it. She knew it. Probably even the walking corpse that was Coop knew it.

He gripped the prisoner's pinky nail with the pliers, digging the tip deep under the nail bed. He watched Coop from the corner of his eye, ready to react if Coop let go, if he fought. But Coop kept holding her hand in place. Of course he did. He was a dead thing, an automaton. All he knew was how to obey.

In one quick jerk, Ryland yanked the nail out by the root.

The soundproof walls deadened the prisoner's scream, but not enough. Her blood coated Coop's hand. Coop flinched away. His throat worked. Ryland watched him, holding his breath.

But Coop kept holding on. He kept obeying. What Ryland had seen hadn't been a bit of his old self coming through – only an instinctive reaction to the blood and the screams. And who *wouldn't* react to that?

But chipped workers weren't supposed to react to anything.

No. He had to stop this – whatever *this* was, wherever these thoughts were coming from. Coop was gone. He had been gone for three years.

You don't really pull people's fingernails out, do you? Coop had asked once, early on, before he had learned Ryland regularly did far worse. *That has to be an exaggeration.* Nervous hope had hidden underneath his flirtatious smile. He hadn't wanted the man he had already gone to bed with by then to be a monster.

The prisoner breathed hard, staring at the bloody pliers. Ryland opened them and let the bloody nail fall to the floor.

"Are you ready to start cooperating?" he asked.

"Cooper," she whispered in a ragged voice. "Please. You can fight this. You can fight *him.*"

If only she knew how many fights the two of them had had. And how little it had gotten either of them in the end.

He took hold of the prisoner's next nail and started to tug, slower this time. Drawing out the pain. The nail offered resistance, but Coop held her hand firmly in place. As he did, though, he looked away. Was that a flash of disgust in his eyes?

You realize you're everything I hate, don't you? Coop had said to him, pulling on his clothes quickly, as if trying to erase the evidence of what they had just done together.

Ryland had flashed him a teasing smile. *And yet you just can't resist me.*

But Coop had met his smile with a scowl. *Don't. Just don't. I can't think about this right now, all right? I can't ... I can't look at you.*

"If you're going to do it," the prisoner spat, "then go ahead and do it."

Ryland blinked away the memory. He came back to the present moment, where he had frozen, no longer pulling at the nail that was still locked in the pliers' grip. Blood seeped out from where the metal had dug under her skin.

He released the nail and let the hand holding the pliers fall to his side. "Go," he ordered Coop. "This will be an easy interrogation. I don't need any help."

"Go where?" Coop asked, face and voice perfectly placid.

"I don't care. Go organize my desk." No doubt he wouldn't be able to find anything when Coop was done. Plus, it meant leaving a chipped worker alone in his office full of secure files for what could turn out to be hours. Back when they had been together, back when Coop had been himself, his feelings for Ryland wouldn't have been enough to stop him from taking advantage of that opportunity. Just like Ryland's feelings for Coop had never been enough to get him to leave his job.

But he would have. He *would* have. Just as soon as the time was right.

Ryland unlocked the interrogation room door. Coop walked away without a second glance.

Ryland slammed the door shut after him. He turned back to the prisoner, raising the pliers again. Why was it so damned hot in here? And this shirt – he had never noticed how rough and itchy it was. They just didn't make clothes the way they used to.

"Now," he said to the prisoner, "where were we?"

4

Casey's was a favorite lunch and dinner spot among interrogators, even though the food and ambiance both left a lot to be desired. The burgers were greasy enough to soak through the bottoms of the cheap buns, and the fries always tasted like they had been sitting in stale oil for a few days. The small building was cramped and loud, the tables too close together, with tepid radio hits from twenty years ago blaring through the crackly speakers. But it was right next door to the facility, which meant they did a brisk business, mainly owing to people like Ryland who were too busy or lazy to go farther afield.

Tonight, though, Ryland regretted his choice. The music grated on his nerves, which were already worn thin, and the press of the crowd worsened the feeling of oppressive heat he'd thought he had left behind in the interrogation room. If he hadn't promised Oliver dinner tonight, he would have gone home and tried his luck with whatever he could find in the fridge that wasn't too furry yet.

He looked down at the burger in his hand, and was surprised to find it half gone already. He couldn't remember taking a single bite. The good news was it didn't taste like grease tonight. Probably because everything tasted like sand.

Oliver leaned in to be heard over the blaring music. "You seem ... *off* tonight," he said in his quiet voice. "Is something wrong?"

"I'm sorry," said Ryland. "We came here so I could help you, not so you could watch me sulk over my burger." He set the burger down – he didn't want the rest anyway – and tried to give Oliver his full attention. "Tell me about this prisoner. Did you bring the file?"

Oliver frowned. "Prisoner?"

Ryland wasn't so distracted that he had mixed up the reason for this dinner, was he? "The prisoner," he repeated. "The one you're having so much trouble breaking. That's why you wanted to talk, wasn't it? So I could give you my thoughts?"

"Oh, right. Him." Oliver shook his head ruefully. "I guess you're not the only one who's a little off tonight?" He gave a soft, self-deprecating laugh. It was hard to tell over the noise of the music and the crowd, but Ryland thought his laugh sounded a little strained.

Well, maybe bad days were going around.

He tried to focus all his attention on Oliver, the way Oliver would have done for him. Oliver was the closest friend he had in the facility – maybe the only real friend he had there, or anywhere else. Interrogation was a lonely job. Coop wasn't the only one put off by how Ryland and those like him spent their days. A person didn't have to be on the side of the rebels to be uncomfortable with how the sausage was made. Ryland would have thought that would bond the interrogators closer together – after all, who else did they have? – but in practice, their social muscles were atrophied enough that they kept to themselves.

Oliver was the kind of person someone could pass by every day and not give any more thought than they gave the faded painting of a beach sunset someone had stuck up in the men's bathroom in a vain attempt to brighten the place up. And that was exactly what Ryland had done for years, until they had happened to start talking one day during an escaped-prisoner drill. He hadn't realized until that day just how long Oliver had been working there, and how many prisoners he had successfully broken. His numbers put Ryland's to shame. Maybe there was more to him than Ryland had realized.

Once Ryland started watching him more closely, he saw other things he had overlooked. Like how Oliver was always reading something he thought might help him with his work – most recently, it was a book on some new theory of psychological development. Or how, when someone asked him to do something, no matter how trivial, he would move heaven and earth to get it done. It would have been easy for people to take advantage of him, if anyone had noticed he existed.

And once the two of them had become friends, Ryland found him to be an incredibly loyal and caring confidant. Oliver was the only person he had ever told about Coop – only after Coop was arrested and it was all over, of course. Even then, he had feared the rule-following Oliver would report him for his indiscretion, but to his knowledge, Oliver had never told a soul.

"What do you think?" Oliver asked, bringing him out of his reverie.

Too late, he realized Oliver had been laying out the details of his problem, and Ryland hadn't heard a word. So much for giving Oliver his full attention.

"Hmm," he said, feeling like a terrible friend – as if he needed one more thing to feel bad about today. "That's a tricky situation."

Oliver gave him a wry smile. "You weren't listening, were you?"

Ryland sighed. "I'm sorry. It's been a hell of a day."

Instantly, Oliver's face creased with concern, his own problems apparently forgotten. "What's going on?"

He opened his mouth to give some excuse – a bad night of sleep, a difficult interrogation. But this was Oliver. He had kept Ryland's secret before. He could keep it again.

"The ex-boyfriend I told you about three years ago," he said. He lowered his voice and leaned in toward Oliver. "The rebel."

Oliver's frown grew. "What about him? I thought he was arrested years ago."

"Did you hear about this new chipped-worker trial?"

"I heard a rumor that someone cursed out Norby for suggesting it." Oliver looked half scandalized at that, half secretly envious. "Don't tell me that was *you*."

"That's an exaggeration," said Ryland, "but not much of one. Also, it was more than a suggestion. He delivered the chipped worker straight to my office."

Ryland could tell Oliver had put the pieces together when Oliver's mouth went round with shock. "And it's that ex of yours?"

"Yes. No. I don't know." Ryland rested his elbows on the table and his head in his hands. Why had he thought talking about it might make it *easier*? "The chip – it takes away most of who they were. The voice is the same. The face. But that's about it. He assisted me in an interrogation. He didn't fight. Didn't argue. That alone is enough to tell me there's nothing of him left in there."

"Have you reported the conflict of interest?"

"And put it on the record that I was sharing my bed with a rebel for two years? That I knew what he was and never turned him in?"

"You don't have to get that specific with it," said Oliver. "Say he was your neighbor. A friend of a friend. Or confess to the one-night stand – you said that's how it started, didn't you?"

Ryland had forgotten he had shared that much with Oliver. "It's not necessary," he said shortly. "It's not *him*. I just need to remember that." He looked up to meet Oliver's eyes. "I can handle it."

Oliver blinked and drew back. Ryland hadn't realized his look had been that intense. "All right, all right," said Oliver with a nervous laugh. "I never doubted that, you know. I was thinking about *you*. About you having to work with him every day. To see him like ... that."

"It's not him," Ryland repeated.

"Why put yourself through that?" Oliver shook his head. "He was out of your life. It was for the best. Better to keep it that way."

Why, indeed? Ryland didn't have an answer. He hadn't wanted a chipped worker in the first place, even before he had found out who that worker was. If he took Oliver's advice, what would he be losing?

Coop. Only Coop. All over again.

"You're right." The music jangled in his ears. He glared up at the speaker in the corner. "Sorry about this, but I think we'll need to take a rain check. My head's not in the right place tonight."

A flash of hurt crossed Oliver's face, gone almost too quickly for Ryland to notice. But it was visible long enough to make Ryland feel even worse.

"It's all right," Oliver assured him. "Listen – why don't we go out tonight? Somewhere more exciting than here. We could have some fun. Take your mind off things."

Ryland blinked at him. "I'm sorry – did you suggest going someplace *exciting*?" Oliver's idea of excitement was getting chocolate ice cream instead of vanilla.

"You're always saying I should get out more," said Oliver. "That it would be good for me to have some fun once in a while – the kind that doesn't involve sitting alone on my couch with a movie I've seen a dozen times. Well, maybe tonight is 'every once in a while.' What do you say?" He offered Ryland a tentative smile.

His words had the annoying benefit of being true. Worse, Ryland was hardly one to talk – he had been even worse than Oliver in that regard since Coop. These days, his version of fun didn't even involve his couch and a movie. It looked more like catching up on paperwork after dinner and then turning in early. He could benefit from taking his own advice, and he knew it.

But he shook his head. The thought of a crowded bar or club made his head throb with an anticipatory headache. "Another time, maybe. I don't feel up to it tonight. Besides, you should probably focus on working out your strategy for that prisoner."

"If you don't feel up to going out," Oliver said, "you could come back to my apartment for a while." He gave a tense little shrug. "It would be quieter than going out – and it would be better than going back home and brooding. I've even got a bottle we could break open, if you're looking to distract yourself the old-fashioned way. I've been saving it."

He held his body perfectly still, like he was bracing for a blow and not a simple yes or no.

Realization hit Ryland like a gallon of ice water straight to his gut. The invitation to go out, when Oliver never went out. The offer to open up a bottle he had been saving – and why, just because Ryland was having a bad day? And then there was how Oliver had practically forgotten the reason he had invited Ryland out to Casey's in the first place.

No. Oliver wasn't ... he couldn't be *interested* in him. Not like that.

But they'd been having more and more nights like this, hadn't they? Casual dinners where Ryland helped Oliver work through a thorny issue with one interrogation or another. Ryland hadn't thought much of it – that was the kind of thing friends did for each other. He certainly hadn't thought about the fact that Oliver had far more successful interrogations under his belt than Ryland did. What did he need Ryland's help for?

And when was the last time Oliver had gone on a date? Not for ... oh, half a year or so, at least. Around the same time Oliver had started asking him for more help with his interrogations. That hadn't caught Ryland's attention, either – after all, it had been much longer than that for him.

Oliver was still watching him, waiting for his response. The hope in his eyes, now that Ryland knew what to look for, was painfully raw and desperate.

Ryland cursed silently to himself.

He knew how selfish it made him that his first thought was, *As if I need this right now, on top of everything else.* Now he was going to have to figure out how to let Oliver down gently, and do it without destroying their friendship in the process – the only real friendship Ryland had. And he had to do it while his head was too full of Coop to focus on anything else.

He opened his mouth. Closed it again. No. No, he couldn't do this. Not right now.

He glanced over his shoulder at the door. His body screamed with the urge to get out of here, now, this instant. Away from the hope and fear in Oliver's eyes.

He stood so hard his chair squealed across the floor. "I'm sorry," he said again. "I need to get home. Take an early night. Everything that's happened today ... I need to crawl into bed and start over fresh tomorrow."

Another flash of hurt in Oliver's eyes, gone almost before Ryland could see it.

Ryland turned away, his heart pounding with the need to escape, and fled before Oliver could protest.

5

—·—

Entering the facility this late at night, Ryland had to resist the urge to avoid the harsh floodlights and creep along in the shadows. He felt like a criminal, even though he had left the facility at a later hour than this on many a long workday. He had every right to be here, at any hour he chose.

And it wasn't as if anyone would see him, even if he *had* been doing something he shouldn't have. At this time of night, all the security was automated. And the automated security wouldn't be a problem, because Ryland had set it to delete any footage where he would appear for the next several hours. Which, again, was something he was perfectly entitled to do. He had been given that ability the day he had moved up from the junior-interrogator position. There were plenty of legitimate reasons, after all, why an interrogator might not want to show up on an official recording. Some prisoners needed more coercion than the official rulebook allowed, even though the rules gave them plenty of leeway. And other prisoners needed to quietly disappear.

Even if anyone found out he had been here tonight – which they wouldn't – no one would question his actions. There was no reason for him to skulk along in the shadows like a rebel on a mission.

And yet, as he crept up the stone steps and entered the code that would allow him inside at this hour, he still found himself hunching his shoulders, turning away from the places where he knew the cameras were hidden.

The building was eerie at this time of night. Only the emergency lights were on – the main lighting had switched off at midnight to save power. The emergency lights cast the familiar hallway in a dim yellow. Ryland peered around every corner, rehearsing excuses in his head just in case an interrogator working late happened across him and wanted to know what he was doing. Not that he needed an excuse. Any interrogator would assume he was working on a difficult prisoner, just as he would assume the same of them.

They would have no reason to think he was doing anything wrong.

He *wasn't* doing anything wrong.

Where had Norby told him the chipped worker would be stored at night? He scrolled through his messages until he found the location. A repurposed storage room on the maintenance level, where Ryland rarely had reason to go. He found the room at the end of a long hallway. The door was locked, but Norby had given him the code.

The room was almost as bare as an interrogation room. Darker patches on the faded gray walls showed where the shelves had been hastily removed. In their place, six bunks had been built into the wall – three sets of two, upper and lower. The bunks looked like shelves themselves, but big enough to store humans rather than cleaning supplies.

Apparently Norby had high hopes for the chipped-worker trial. But for now, only one of the bunks was occupied. On the bottom bunk against the far wall, a figure lay curled with his knees to his chest and his face to the wall.

Coop had always slept like that. *Curled up like a pillbug*, Ryland used to tease him. Coop, in turn, had griped about Ryland's habit of stretching out like a starfish to fill every inch of any bed he slept in – *As if I have any control over what I do while I'm sleeping*, Ryland had protested.

Ryland should have been asleep right now. He had tried. After hours of tossing and turning, drifting into and out of nightmares about Coop's blood and Coop's screams, he had given up. He had come here instead.

Ryland rested a soft hand on Coop's shoulder. Coop used to startle awake, sometimes throwing a half-asleep punch at whoever was unlucky enough to be the one to wake him. But this version of Coop uncurled slowly from his pillbug shape and sat up to meet Ryland's gaze with placid, empty eyes.

"Good morning," said Coop, as if Ryland hadn't just awakened him in the middle of the night. "What do you need?"

39

"I need ... " What *did* he need? What had made him think coming here was a good idea? Sleep deprivation, no doubt. He knew the effects it had on the brain. He used it on his prisoners often enough.

He sat down heavily on the edge of Coop's bed, ducking his head to keep it from banging on the upper bunk. "I need to talk to you."

"What would you like to talk about?"

"Would you stop talking like that?"

"I'm sorry. Please explain, and I'll do my best. Talking like what?"

Ryland buried his head in his hands. "You and me," he said, his voice muffled by his fingers. "We shared a bed for *two years*. For most of that time, we shared a lot more than that." Dreams. Secrets. Ryland had planned to leave his job for him, for god's sake. To leave his entire *life*.

"I'm sorry," said Coop. "Intimate relationships aren't allowed under the terms of the agreement."

Ryland made a strangled sound. "I'm talking about before. You had a life before this. *We* had a life. You can't tell me you don't remember any of that."

"I'm sorry. I don't know what you'd like me to do. Can you be clearer?"

"We met at a club, of all places," Ryland said into his hands, remembering the throbbing music and the sticky smell of booze like it was yesterday. "I never went to clubs. Neither did you, but

I didn't know that then. I was coming off the bad end of a worse relationship. You were there to meet a resistance contact."

In Coop, who had stood off to the side and shyly watched the action from under his floppy curls, Ryland had seen the antidote to the sharp-edged lover whose angles had finally cut him one too many times. In Ryland, Coop had seen ... what? Ryland had asked himself that question many times. He still didn't know.

He looked up, hoping to see some trace of recognition on Coop's face. He saw nothing but emptiness.

"Your name came up in an interrogation a week later," said Ryland. "I erased the recording. It was a stupid impulse – I regretted it as soon as I did it." But he hadn't regretted it nearly as much as he had known he should have.

He had told himself it was simple self-preservation, a way to avoid any blowback from his unfortunate indiscretion the previous week. He hadn't known about Coop's resistance involvement when they had met at the club, of course, but still. That was the kind of thing that could come back to bite somebody in the ass.

If it had ended there, he might have been able to go on believing his own excuses.

Instead, he had tracked Coop down using the facility's resources. It had made him feel like a stalker – Coop hadn't given him his address or contact information, and that had clearly been by choice. He had knocked on Coop's front door and come clean about who he was, where he worked, what he did. He had told Coop about the prisoner's confession, had told him to be careful – to cut all ties with the resistance as soon as he could.

And they had mutually agreed to end their brief association then and there – to forget about their night together and move on with their lives.

Coop hadn't cut ties with the resistance. And neither of them had moved on.

"It lasted two years, before you were arrested," he said, studying Coop's blank eyes. "Two *years*, Coop. There has to be some trace of that left in your mind." There had to be some trace of Ryland. Some trace of *Coop*.

"I'm sorry." Coop's voice was empty of regret, empty of sympathy, empty of anything. "I don't know how to give you what you want."

Ryland didn't know what came over him at that moment. Maybe it was the sleep deprivation. Or the strange yellow lighting, messing with his head. All he knew was that without his conscious volition, he was leaning in, closing the narrow space between him and Coop. Pressing his lips to Coop's. Kissing him.

His lips felt just the same as Ryland remembered. Plump and whisper-soft, with a faint herbal taste Ryland couldn't place. For a split second, letting his eyes drift shut, Ryland could pretend. He could forget.

But Coop's lips didn't open to meet his. And when Ryland drew back, Coop's eyes were still wide open.

"I'm sorry," said Coop, "but intimate touching isn't allowed."

Shame crawled in Ryland's gut like a living thing. "You have nothing to apologize for," he said roughly. "I'm the one who's sorry. I shouldn't have..." He shook his head hard, trying to clear it of the memory of his lips on Coop's, so familiar, so horribly wrong.

"Please," he said. "Please just tell me you remember *something*."

"I remember," said Coop.

Ryland went still. "What..." The word came out as a croak. His voice wasn't working properly anymore. "What do you remember?"

"You wanted me to tell you I remembered something," said Coop in that terrible flat voice, "and so I did. What would you like me to remember?"

Of course. Ryland had given him an order – or that was how his words had registered in Coop's chipped brain. And Coop had obeyed. Of course he had.

He stood quickly, narrowly avoiding bashing the back of his head on the top bunk. "Nothing," he said without looking at Coop. "I have to go."

He couldn't stay here one second longer. He couldn't come back to work tomorrow morning knowing Coop was here waiting for him. He had to do what Oliver had suggested. Declare the conflict of interest. Let the technology division take Coop back. Banish this ghost once and for all.

"Goodbye," he said, willing his voice not to break. He told himself not to turn around, not to give Coop one last look. He did anyway.

Where would Coop go after this? Ryland imagined him standing anonymous on an assembly line, pulling levers, tightening bolts. Alive out there somewhere – if this even counted as life. Ryland didn't see how it could. And yet his mind screamed at him that Coop would be alive – that he would never again be able to tell himself Coop was long gone, a closed chapter in his life. Coop would be alive, and Ryland would never know where.

Ryland would never see him again.

The night he had shown up unexpectedly on Coop's doorstep and given his confession, they had agreed that this would be the last time they would see each other. Even if they had wanted to try to build something between them, even if there had been no risk, Ryland had known he would never again be able to look at Coop without seeing the face of a rebel. Someone who would rather see the world fall into anarchy than live with the knowledge that someone, somewhere, was doing something that offended his precious moral sensibilities. And Coop, he knew, would never be able to look at him without seeing a monster.

Ryland had offered Coop his hand to shake, like it was a business deal. Coop had wrinkled his upturned nose, making the freckles on his cheeks shift into new constellations. *I hate shaking hands,* he had said.

Their eyes had met.

Ryland hadn't left. Not until the sun was crawling red-eyed up from the horizon.

That had been the beginning of the end. The first bad decision that would spawn a thousand more.

He had felt the truth of that then. And he felt it now, as he held his hand out to Coop like he had that day on his doorstep.

"Come with me," he said. "Quickly." Before he could have a chance to think about what he was doing.

Coop stood and took his hand. His fingers were cold in Ryland's. "Where are we going?"

"Somewhere you've never been," Ryland answered. Not in all the time they had been together.

Ryland's house.

6

— · —

Ryland walked Coop in through his back door, under a wide-brimmed hat and draped in an oversized coat. There shouldn't be any cameras around back, but the ones watching the street had probably glimpsed Coop for a few seconds – and Ryland, carrying the disguise out. Would Ryland's bundle of clothes register as suspicious? Had Coop looked up, even for a second?

Ryland urged Coop inside with a gentle hand on his back, and quickly swung the door shut behind them both. He cleared his throat. "Well," he said, "this is it."

Coop stood still, staring straight ahead of him at Ryland's entryway, the floor polished to a mirror shine by the cleaner who had come in yesterday. Beyond the entryway lay the living room, which suddenly seemed much too large for one man living alone. And could Coop see how much he had spent on the furniture, and on that plush carpet which now seemed like a ridiculous expense? Past the living room, a glimpse of the kitchen was visible, full of fancy high-end appliances Ryland never used.

Yes, this is what an interrogator's salary buys me, he wanted to say. *Yes, they pay me very well to rip out fingernails. But you already knew that.*

"Well?" he said instead, more irritably than he meant to. "Are you going to say anything?"

Coop turned to face him, his expression as placid as ever. "What would you like me to say?"

Ryland forced himself to take a breath. Coop wasn't standing there judging him. Coop *couldn't* judge him, not with the sliver of brain the technology division had left him. He was simply waiting for orders.

"Nothing," Ryland said, already feeling ashamed of himself. This was not starting off well. "You can take off that hat. And that coat."

Coop did as Ryland had suggested, hanging them both carefully on the hook by the door. Then he went back to standing with his arms pressed to his sides, staring at nothing.

"Sit," Ryland urged. Then, when Coop began to lower himself as if to sit down right there on the floor, he hastily pointed to the living room. "There. On the couch."

Coop obeyed, sitting with his back straight and his hands neatly folded in his lap. Was he comfortable? He didn't look it. Did he even care about being comfortable? Did he care that he was here and not assisting Ryland in another interrogation? Maybe it was all the same to him.

He ducked into the kitchen and poured Coop a glass of cool water, grateful for the respite from looking at Coop's empty face. But if he hadn't wanted to look at Coop, he shouldn't have brought him *here*, right? Rather than stop too long to think about that, he hurried back out to the living room, glass in hand.

He pressed it into Coop's hands. Coop took it without complaint. Ryland imagined he would have accepted the pliers the same way, if Ryland had handed them to him and told him to start pulling out fingernails.

"Drink," Ryland told him when Coop didn't do anything with the glass. Immediately, Coop tilted it to his lips. Ryland really was going to have to tell him to do everything, wasn't he?

The thought of sitting next to him at a stiff and polite distance, like an estranged couple trying to pretend they didn't hate each other, was unbearable. Ryland stayed standing instead. *Hovering*, if he was honest with himself. "Do you need anything to eat?"

"I can safely go without food for three days and remain productive," Coop answered, "but it's not recommended to let me go that long on a regular basis."

A small shudder rippled through Ryland. He turned away before Coop could say anything else. "I'll find you something."

That turned out to be easier said than done. The sum total of his fridge contents turned out to be a bottle of ketchup, a jar of pickles, and a container filled with some fuzzy green substance that might have been food at one point. A search through the cabinets yielded a single bag of microwave popcorn and a box of stale crackers.

But that wasn't a problem. He could order something for both of them. He frowned at the window, where the moon was still visible in the black velvet sky. Not at this hour of the night, he couldn't. And even once morning came, could he risk a delivery person coming to the door? A single glimpse of Coop would be disastrous. If he went to pick something up instead, could he risk leaving Coop here alone?

The moon stared in at him like a nosy neighbor. He hastily pulled the blinds closed, then hurried through the house, doing the same for all the windows. This was a highly surveilled area. If a neighbor or delivery person didn't catch a glimpse of Coop, it was only a matter of time before a streetlamp camera or patrolling drone did. How was he going to pull this off long-term?

What, exactly, had he been thinking?

He returned to the living room empty-handed. He paced back and forth across the expensive carpet, restless as a prisoner in a cell. What had he done? What was he *going* to do?

This wasn't like him. He wasn't a pacer, wasn't one to let his thoughts run away with him. But then, he normally wasn't the kind of person who would steal government property or secret a potential security risk away in his home, either.

If his anxious pacing bothered Coop at all, Coop gave no sign. He kept on sipping at his water. When the glass was empty, he asked, "What would you like me to do next?"

Coop's voice, soft though it was, seemed explosively loud in the silence. Loud enough to be overheard. Ryland glanced at the living room window, the blinds now tightly shut. In the morning, that oversized window, looking directly out at the road where all the neighbors walked their dogs, would be a threat he didn't know how to handle. For now, no one would be suspicious if the blinds stayed closed. It was the middle of the night. Everyone would expect him to be asleep, blinds shut to block out the light.

"Asleep," said Ryland aloud. "You should sleep." It was then that it occurred to Ryland that he didn't have a guest room – and why would he, when he never had guests? It didn't matter. He would sleep on the couch.

Coop frowned. "I thought you brought me here to work."

I brought you here because apparently I'm a sentimental idiot. And wouldn't everyone at work be surprised if they knew? His strong stomach in interrogations was the stuff of legend. "It's nighttime. I want you to get some rest. I want you to ... " *I want you to wake up as yourself.* But that wouldn't happen.

Ryland forced himself to still his pacing. "I want you to keep yourself hidden," he said. "Don't look out the windows. Don't answer the door. If you see anyone but me, if you hear anyone but me, you hide. Got it?"

Coop nodded. "If I see anyone but you, if I hear anyone but you, I hide," he parroted.

Ryland's eyes slid away from Coop. Seeing Coop here in his living room, on his couch, felt *wrong*. It wasn't even because of Coop's corpselike stare. Well, not *only* because of that.

It was because, for two years, he had been so careful to keep Coop away from this place.

By mutual agreement, they had stayed away from each other's homes after that one night Ryland had shown up unexpectedly at Coop's door. For security reasons – or that was what they had told each other and themselves. It could be a death sentence for Coop if anyone looked too closely at his relationship with Ryland. And the same was true for Ryland if the resistance got wind of what was happening between the two of them – undoubtedly they wouldn't assume Ryland's intentions were pure.

That was a sensible enough reason to rent a separate apartment just for their nights together. But it wasn't the only reason. They just never talked about the others aloud.

If Coop had let Ryland into his home, it would have meant admitting how comfortable he was getting with the enemy. Even as their relationship evolved far beyond the physical, even as their late-night conversations grew more and more intimate, keeping a separate apartment made it easy to pretend a certain distance existed between them. Coop didn't have to say it aloud for Ryland to understand this. Ryland knew what Coop thought of him.

And if Ryland had brought Coop home, he might have had to see the look on his face when Coop saw the luxuries that interrogating his resistance friends had bought him. Ryland might have had to think about how he was spending his nights in bed with a rebel while he spent his days working against everything they stood for. And once he'd had one of them in his home, would he still be able to go into work the next morning and treat every other rebel as a nameless, faceless source of information?

Maybe he had been afraid to find out.

"I wasn't ashamed of you," he said to Coop now. "That was never it. And I would gladly have shared my life with you, if things had been different. They were *going* to be different. I really did buy us a place to live together. I know you thought I was lying about that, but I wasn't." He sighed, thinking about the little cabin with its old-fashioned wood stove. Coop would have loved it. "I wish you could have seen it."

"I'm sorry," Coop said. "I don't understand."

"It's okay. You don't have to. I shouldn't have said anything." Coop wasn't here to be a dumping ground for Ryland's guilty conscience.

Why *was* Coop here?

He couldn't go on like this forever, with Coop hidden in his house like a fugitive. Sitting empty-headed on his couch, waiting for orders. Ryland wasn't sure he could go on like this for one more day.

But he couldn't go back in time and undo his foolish impulse. So what was his way forward?

"I'm going to find a way to help you," said Ryland. "I'm going to find a way to bring you back."

After that, if Coop wanted nothing more to do with him, that was his choice. Just so long as he was Coop again.

Coop shook his head. "It's my job to assist *you* with whatever you need," he corrected. "Do you have a job for me?"

A headache began to form behind Ryland's eyes. He rubbed his temples. "Sleep," he said. "Just sleep."

"All right," said Coop, and promptly curled into his pillbug shape on the couch. With his face turned to the back of the couch, he closed his eyes. Within seconds, his breathing took on the steady rhythm of sleep.

Ryland stared.

"I guess I'm going to have to learn to be more precise," he said as he bent to take Coop into his arms. He would carry him to the bedroom, and take the couch himself.

But before he could touch Coop, his phone rang. "There's been a security breach," Norby said as soon as he answered, without so much as a hello. "You need to come in right away. The chipped worker is gone."

7

— · —

Ryland entered the facility and walked into a whirlwind. Every inch of the lobby was full of grim-faced people in security uniforms – barking orders, talking on headsets, scanning walls and floors with arcane devices. Ryland had never seen this kind of frenzy in the facility before dawn. He couldn't remember seeing this kind of frenzy in the facility *ever*. He needed a cup of coffee.

Or maybe, he thought with a chill, what he needed was to head right on back out the door before anyone noticed him. When he had gotten the call and weighed the risks of leaving Coop in his house alone, he had thought about how not obeying Norby's summons would make him look suspicious. Only now did he wonder whether someone had already figured out the truth. Easier to get him to come in on his own than to send someone to arrest him, after all.

He took a step backward, reaching for the door. But at that moment, Norby emerged from the maelstrom, his eyes locking on Ryland. "You got here quickly."

With an inner sigh, Ryland stepped forward, away from his escape route. "You said it was urgent."

"That's an understatement. The facility was breached. Our first breach in more than a decade." Norby closed the distance between them. Gone was his usual affable demeanor. From the look on his face, he was about ready to step into an interrogation room and start ripping out fingernails himself.

"And you," he said, "were here when it happened."

Ryland's heart froze in his chest before coming back to life to slam painfully against his rib cage. His mind raced, his thoughts swirling and fizzing away before he could grab onto any of them. Run? No, he wouldn't stand a chance – not with the facility swarming with security. Give himself up and hope for mercy? Yeah, right. He had worked here too long to expect any mercy from this place.

Deny everything, then. For as long as he could.

He had met many a prisoner who had made that same decision. It never ended well for them.

Norby's brow creased at Ryland's lack of response. "You *were* here," he repeated, a hint of uncertainty in his voice now. "Weren't you? Your car was, at least. The parking garage cameras caught your plates."

His car. A weakness in the system he had never considered. The mechanism that automatically deleted any footage with his face in it would only work if the cameras actually *saw* his face. On his way into and out of the garage, they might not have. And his plates were on file with the facility, allowing him to enter the garage without a security screening.

"It's all right," said Norby, his voice surprisingly mild for someone who was about to have him arrested. "I'll make sure that part stays out of the official files as much as possible. I know you used the privacy codes. Probably working on the Capshaw interrogation, am I right? I know there were some ... irregularities in that file."

Irregularities, in this context, meaning a discrepancy between the official goals for the interrogation and what had *actually* been asked of him. In this case, someone high up wanted this prisoner's confession to happen off-the-record. Ryland didn't know why. He didn't care. But right now, that fact might just save his ass.

Ryland cleared his throat, trying to recover his composure and his voice. "That's right. I've found it's best to handle those cases late at night, for the sake of discretion."

Norby let out an audible sigh of relief. "You're a lifesaver, Eskell," he said. "That's the best news I've heard all morning."

Ryland frowned. "I don't follow."

"Just a few minutes after your car left the garage, the night janitor came in to clean the room where the chipped worker was being stored, saw it was empty, and raised the alarm. Unless the intruders moved impossibly fast, they were here at the same time as you. Which means you might have seen something out of the ordinary. Something that could help us catch whoever did this."

Ryland steadied his breathing, trying to slow his racing heart. He hadn't been found out.

Not yet.

"I didn't see anything," he said with a shake of his head. "I'm sorry."

"Security will want to talk to you anyway," Norby said. "They've been very eager to talk to the only potential eyewitness." Before Ryland could protest, he made a broad beckoning gesture over his shoulder.

Almost immediately, two uniformed security officers emerged from the crowd, as if they had been waiting for this signal. They could have been twins – sharp, angular, with dour faces and crow-black eyes. Their hair was the only meaningful difference between them – one had dark chestnut curls cropped close to his head, while the other had a striking shock of white-blond hair.

"Ryland Eskell?" Chestnut asked. Those crow eyes looked sharp enough to slice through him and all his excuses.

Ryland managed a faint nod, not trusting himself to speak.

"The eyewitness," Blondie added.

"Not exactly." Ryland forced the words from his mouth. "I didn't see – "

"We've been waiting to talk to you," said Chestnut, turning on his heel. "You're the best lead we've got. Follow me." He was already walking away.

Blondie brought up the rear, striding forward until Ryland had to hurry after Chestnut or risk the other man slamming into him. Refusing clearly wasn't an option. They didn't handcuff him like a prisoner, or drag him down the hallway by his arms, but they might as well have.

They sat him down in a small, unfriendly meeting room dominated by a long table. The two of them sat at one end, Ryland at the other. Staring into their sharp eyes, Ryland wondered if this was how his prisoners felt.

"Can you tell us when you arrived at the facility, and when you left?" Chestnut asked. "Don't worry – this will be kept out of the official record, as requested by Mr. Norby."

"I'm sure you have that information already, in the recordings from the parking garage." Ryland tried not to fidget – squirming in his chair would make him look guilty – but that left him sitting frozen, too stiff and awkward to be innocent.

"Yes," said Chestnut, "but we'd like your corroboration. In the interest of thoroughness."

Or to make sure he wasn't lying. Ryland gave the approximate times as best he could remember – although the clock had been the last thing on his mind last night. His voice sounded high and false to his own ears. Blondie took out a tablet and began making notes.

"And where in the facility did you go while you were here?" asked Chestnut.

"Prisoner Capshaw's cell. The interrogation room. That's it." They wouldn't be able to tell where in the footage the missing recordings had been – could they? He had been promised the system handled the erasures too smoothly for that, filling in the blank spaces with footage from earlier in the feed. But no one had mentioned the garage loophole, either.

"Nowhere else?" Chestnut pressed.

"I might have visited the bathroom at one point."

Blondie made a note of that. "Did the chipped worker assist you in the interrogation?" Chestnut asked.

"No, I didn't ask for his help."

"Why not?" Chestnut asked.

Ryland shrugged. "I'm not used to him yet. And the tech who delivered him told me to make sure his physical needs were met. I assume that includes sleep." Ryland's voice didn't falter.

Chestnut nodded. His face gave no clue to his thoughts. "While you were in the building," he said, "did you see or hear anything unusual?"

Ryland shook his head. "Nothing. I'm sorry."

Chestnut leaned forward. His crow eyes seemed to pierce through Ryland. "Are you sure? Nothing at all?"

Were his denials making him look more suspicious? He couldn't read the security officers' faces, couldn't discern the intent behind their questions. They could have been an inch away from arresting him, and he wouldn't know until it was too late. Was this why his prisoners got so weird in the head so soon, even before he started in with the pliers and the electricity?

"I don't think so." Ryland paused, pretended to think. "Well ... I might have heard something."

Chestnut leaned in further across the table. Blondie stopped his note-taking, his gaze intent. "Like what?" Chestnut asked.

"Footsteps, maybe. I didn't think anything of it. I assumed it was another interrogator." Was he saving himself, or only digging a deeper grave for himself?

The questions flew hard and fast after that.

Where in the building did you hear these footsteps?

What time was it?

Were they slow or quick? Heavy or light? Did they sound like they belonged to a man or a woman?

With every lie Ryland told, he felt the noose around his neck draw tighter. As an interrogator, he would have seen through these lies in a heartbeat.

Finally, Blondie tucked the tablet away. "I think we're done here," said Chestnut, rising to his feet.

"Then ... I can go?" Ryland tried not to sound too anxious about the answer. Only someone afraid of being found out would have anything to fear. He schooled his face into an expression of mild annoyance, like a man who had work to do and was being kept from it.

"I'm sorry," said Chestnut.

Ryland tensed, waiting for them to advance on him. For the click of the handcuffs as they settled around his wrists.

"Yours is the only evidence we have to go on so far." Did Chestnut look ... nervous? "And please take no offense, but I'm afraid it's not much. We'll do what we can to find the chipped worker and the cause of this breach, but it may take some time."

"We will, of course, work day and night until we find the ones who did this," Blondie added. "We understand the seriousness of a breach of this magnitude."

Slowly, the pieces of the puzzle rearranged themselves in Ryland's head. He wasn't a suspect here. They weren't trying to intimidate him. The sharpness in their eyes, the intensity of their questions, was their way of impressing upon him – the interrogator with a reputation for brutality – how seriously they took this crime against him.

They were afraid of *him*.

Had they ever even considered suspecting him? Had anyone? Or did his position place him above suspicion?

"But I can go," Ryland reiterated. He didn't make it a question this time.

Chestnut nodded. The nerves on his face were clear, now that Ryland knew what to look for. "You can go."

Ryland stepped back into the maelstrom. As he shoved past the swarming security officers, he noted the wary glances they gave him, and how quickly they tried to step out of his way. They raised their voices conspicuously as they passed, so he could hear what they were saying and be assured that they were hard at work.

– a manual review of all recordings from the entire facility –

– pull all streetlamp camera and drone feeds within a twenty-block radius –

– door-to-door searches aren't out of the question –

He paused at that last one, frowning at the security officer who had spoken. "Isn't that a bit of an overreaction?"

The man shook his head. "Not at all," he said. "Rebels have breached one of the most secure facilities in existence. This is an existential threat, interrogator. We understand that as well as you do."

Ryland nodded and tried to look reassured. Inside, he felt anything but.

Door-to-door searches. Every camera feed gone over with a fine-toothed comb. The nation's entire security apparatus closing in to battle an existential threat.

It was only a matter of time before someone found a clue. The tiniest thing could be enough to lead back to Ryland. Looking around at the swarm, Ryland had a sinking feeling it would happen sooner rather than later.

Restoring Coop to his former self wouldn't be enough. Ryland had only two choices now.

Either bring Coop back, with some plausible excuse for what had happened to him ...

Or finally keep his promise to Coop, and give up everything for a life as a fugitive.

8

— • —

That night, after the security swarm was long gone and the building lay still and quiet, Ryland snuck Coop in the same way he had snuck him out last night.

This time, it wasn't as easy as only entering the code that would automatically delete the camera footage. There were guards at every door, even the emergency tunnel that exited a block away. So Ryland went through the front, like a man who had nothing to hide.

Coop walked in beside him. He wore a suit to match Ryland's, and a hat that covered as much of his face as he could get away with while still looking natural. When Ryland flashed his ID to the guard, Coop did the same. It was an old expired ID of Ryland's that he had never gotten around to shredding, but the guards didn't look closely enough to tell the difference. They recognized Ryland, after all, and Ryland was above suspicion.

Ryland knew the position of every hidden camera in the hallway, and as he and Coop passed, he turned to give each one a full view of his face. It was counterintuitive, and made him feel prickles of unease down the back of his neck, but he needed to make sure they got a good view of him. He had entered the code before coming inside, and he needed all this footage erased.

When he led Coop into the interrogation room, Coop didn't hesitate, and offered no word of protest. Nor did he object when Ryland, his voice threatening to break, ordered him to sit in the central metal chair. He sat immediately, and looked up at Ryland with an expressionless face, waiting for his next orders. No fear in his eyes. No betrayal.

"I'm sorry," said Ryland as he fastened the restraints – not because he thought Coop would go anywhere, but because he needed to make sure he wouldn't fall and hurt himself. He said it again as he lifted Coop's shirt to place the electrodes. His hands trembled against Coop's warm skin. How many times had he run his fingers down Coop's chest? How many times had he felt Coop shiver against him? Now Coop's flesh gave no response. Warm though it was, it might as well have been the flesh of a corpse.

Coop looked down at the electrodes, his face betraying only mild curiosity. "Sorry about what?"

Ryland couldn't bring himself to answer.

Coop would find out soon enough.

Electricity would short out the chip, Norby had said. His own research confirmed it. He had spent every spare moment studying today, under the guise of doing background research on one of his prisoners. While the hallways had bustled with tense-faced security officers, and fellow interrogators had shared their theories about the breach in hushed tones, Ryland had sat at his desk, reading about chipped workers.

Oliver had knocked on his office door while he was reading. Ryland had blown him off with a few terse words about being busy with prisoner research. It was only after Oliver had left that Ryland had realized this was the first time they had talked since Ryland had run out of Casey's in a sweaty panic.

He had gone looking for Oliver, intending to apologize, but Oliver had already been in the middle of his next interrogation. It might have been for the best, because with Coop still occupying his every thought, Ryland had no room to figure out what to say. Later, when this was over, he would find a way to make it up to Oliver.

Norby had said shorting out the chip would take enough electricity that it was bound to kill the worker in the process. But now Ryland knew that wasn't necessarily true. He knew electricity. He knew how much the average prisoner could take. The ranges in the research were survivable ... maybe ... at least for a young and healthy subject. And it *was* a range, and a fairly broad one, at that. Maybe Coop's chip wouldn't require the maximum amount to short it out.

Anyway, this method was safer than amateur brain surgery, which had been his other option.

Ryland attached the last of the electrodes and stepped back. He looked down at his hands and willed them to stop shaking.

He tried to tell himself it was only an interrogation. He had done this hundreds of times.

"What do you need me to do?" Coop asked.

It took Ryland a moment to find his voice. "I need you to trust me," he said. "No matter what happens. This ... " His voice caught. "This is going to hurt."

"As a chipped worker, I can endure more pain than the average human," Coop said. "But you're required by contract to provide all necessary medical treatment."

How many of those canned speeches had the techs implanted in him? Ryland shuddered as he stepped back to the controls built into the wall. The wires attached to the electrodes disappeared into the shiny metal square like a tangle of snakes.

He turned the dial up to the minimum amount that would be required to short out a chip. Even that amount of electricity was more than he would ordinarily have used on a prisoner – unless he was sure it was worth the risk of them dying under interrogation.

"I'm sorry," Ryland said again, and pressed the button.

He held it down for a count of five. One – and Coop's muscles went rigid, his back arching. Two – his mouth gaped open, his frozen lungs trying to remember how to scream. Three – his scream ripped through the air. Four – the scream faded to a thin and ragged whimper. Five – and then Ryland let go, and Coop sagged back into the chair like a puppet with its strings cut.

His chin dropped to his chest. He was suddenly, terribly silent. Ryland rushed to him. "Coop?" Oh god, Coop. "Please tell me you're alive."

"I'm ... alive." Coop didn't raise his head. Full-body shudders ripped through his frame.

Ryland tilted Coop's chin up to meet his eyes. Silent tears ran down Coop's cheeks, but his face was still utterly blank.

"Coop," Ryland said, his voice a desperate whisper, even though he already knew he had failed. "Coop, say something." Maybe there would be a delayed reaction. Maybe, any second now, Coop would stand up, slap him across the face, and ask what the hell he thought he was doing.

Coop blinked slowly at him. "What would you like me to say?"

Without answering, Ryland let Coop's chin fall. He crossed the room to the controls again and turned the dial up. He rarely risked giving a prisoner a shock this strong, and when he did, he made sure it lasted for one or two seconds at the most.

He didn't let himself hesitate. He pressed the button.

This time, Coop's scream didn't sound human. His arms and legs rattled against the chair hard enough that Ryland was sure there would be bruises later. But if it worked, the bruises wouldn't matter. And if he failed ...

If he failed, Coop would be dead, and the bruises wouldn't matter then, either.

He was at three seconds now. Longer than he would have risked for a prisoner. Coop's scream rang through the room in an endless assault of sound, until Ryland wasn't sure if Coop was still screaming, or if his eardrums had given out and all he was hearing was an inner echo that would never fade.

Four seconds. Coop finally ran out of breath. His chest heaved as he struggled to take another. His body jerked and thrashed, the movements frenetic and mechanical.

Five seconds. At last, Ryland let go.

Ryland didn't remember crossing the room to him, but he blinked and then he wasn't standing at the controls anymore. His arms were around Coop, and Coop's sweat was soaking his suit. Coop didn't hug him back. And he didn't push him away. His body was stiff in Ryland's arms as he sucked in ragged breaths.

Still, Ryland tried. "Coop? Coop, talk to me."

Coop tried to lift his chin. It flopped heavily back down to his chest. "I ... I ... " Even his aborted attempts at speech had that terrible flat tone.

"I'm sorry," Ryland murmured against his hair, even though he knew it meant nothing to Coop. "I'm so sorry."

He released Coop. Coop sagged back against the hard metal chair.

Ryland walked back to the controls.

He turned the dial up to the maximum allowable level. He knew of an interrogator who had accidentally killed a prisoner this way. The interrogator had received an official reprimand and a six-week suspension.

Ryland pressed the button.

He mouthed the seconds to himself as he counted. One – Coop's head jerked back so hard Ryland thought his spine might snap. Two – he heard something inside Coop's body crack under the force of his convulsing muscles. Three – Coop's voice gave out at last, his head flopping back and forth, every part of his body twisting and jerking.

Four.

Five.

At the sound of Coop's breathing, Ryland let out his own breath, which he had been holding the whole time. "Coop?"

Coop slowly raised his head. Small trembles ran through him at the effort. His eyes were filled with the red starbursts of burst veins. His cheeks were shiny with tears. "What ... " Coop rasped. "What ... would ... you like me to do?"

No.

No, that had to have worked. It was the highest shock he could deliver. The most it was possible for a prisoner to survive. It was his last chance. Coop's last chance.

It *had* to work.

It hadn't worked.

"I'm sorry," Ryland whispered. The taste of salt met his tongue. He raised a hand to his cheek. It came back wet.

What now? Sneak Coop back out, he supposed, and hope Coop wasn't badly injured enough to draw the guards' attention   . Drive him back home. Sit him back down on his couch and leave him there awaiting orders.

Or ...

He shot a brief glance back at the controls before hastily looking away.

A longer shock might do it. Maybe.

A longer shock might kill him. Probably.

"I wish I could ask you." Ryland tried to focus on Coop through his blurry vision. "This should be your decision. Not mine."

Ryland cast his memory back over every intimate late-night conversation they had shared. But in two years of pillow talk, there had been nothing that gave Ryland a clue as to which Coop would prefer: near-certain death, or a lifetime of *this*.

All Ryland could do was ask himself which option *he* would prefer, and then make a choice he had no right to make.

He turned back to the controls.

He closed his eyes as he pressed the button.

One. He didn't look. Couldn't look.

Two. An aborted scream, then a sudden silence.

Three. The rattle of the restraints against the chair; the dull slap of flesh against metal.

Four. Coop still wasn't screaming.

Five. Ryland didn't open his eyes.

Six. *Please.*

Seven.

Eight.

Nine.

Ten.

He released the button, and he opened his eyes.

Coop sat slumped in the chair, his chin to his chest. He was utterly, terribly still. Ryland couldn't see whether his eyes were open. He couldn't hear him breathing.

"Coop?" Ryland's voice cracked.

Coop didn't stir.

Ryland felt for a pulse. Coop's skin was cold and clammy. He felt nothing, no reassuring drumbeat against his fingers, no matter how faint. Not even a weak, unsteady stirring of life. He held his fingers under Coop's nose. He didn't feel any breath.

He tilted Coop's head up to face him. Coop's eyes were open, unblinking. They stared into his without seeing him.

He had thought Coop had looked like a corpse before. He had been wrong. This was what death looked like.

He didn't allow himself to think, let alone grieve. There would be time for that later. He released Coop and dug in the wall cabinet for the emergency kit. There was a portable defibrillator to restart a prisoner's heart. He had only ever had to use the kit once, during his first year as an interrogator. It hadn't worked. The prisoner had died.

And his hands hadn't been shaking like this then. His mind hadn't been racing like this.

He ripped open Coop's shirt and tore off the electrodes. With hands slick with sweat, he unfastened the restraints and lowered Coop as gently as he could to the floor. He started chest compressions, staring into Coop's waxy face. Hoping. Praying.

Nothing.

When he couldn't stand the feeling of Coop's unresponsive body under his hands anymore, he stopped. He attached the defibrillator pads to Coop's chest, hoping he was remembering the instructions from last year's refresher course correctly. He pressed the shock button. The irony did not escape him.

Back to chest compressions. Then another shock. Nothing.

And another. Nothing.

Finally, he stood.

It was over.

Coop was gone.

"I'm sorry, Coop," he said one last time. He knew it didn't matter. Coop wasn't there anymore to hear him.

Then a gurgling gasp made Ryland jump back. Coop's body jerked as his head snapped up.

"Coop?" Ryland could barely do more than mouth the name.

Coop drew in big, desperate gulps of air. His gaze darted wildly around the room before landing on Ryland.

"Where ... where am I?" He tried to stand, then collapsed bonelessly back to the floor. His red-veined eyes rolled wildly with panic. "Where am I? What *happened*?"

"Coop." It was all Ryland could say, a gasp of relief, a prayer of thanks. "Coop, Coop, Coop." He tasted salt again, but he didn't care, because this time, his tears were tears of relief.

9

—·—

Back home, Coop sat in the same spot at the end of Ryland's couch. But this time, he didn't sit straight-backed and placid, waiting for orders. He hunched over himself like he was a turtle trying to retreat into his shell. His forehead nearly touched his thighs. He curled slightly to the right – that was the side where one of his ribs seemed to be broken after the electric shock session. Tiny tremors ran through him – from the electricity or from the trauma, Ryland couldn't say.

Coop hadn't said a word since they had left the interrogation room.

Ryland sat as close to him as he dared. He wanted nothing more than to wrap his arms around Coop and let Coop melt into him. But he didn't know whether Coop saw him as his rescuer or as the man who had shocked him with so much electricity it had stopped his heart. As the man he had loved or the man who hadn't loved him enough to run away with him.

He rested a gentle hand on Coop's thigh. The muscle went rigid under his fingers. Ryland hastily pulled his hand back. He curled it into a tight ball on his lap.

"It's okay," he murmured. "It's all right. You're safe now."

"Ry." At first, Ryland didn't recognize the whisper for what it was, hearing only a ragged sigh. But that was what Coop used to call him. He was the only one who used a nickname for him, the only one for whom he was anything other than *Ryland* or *Interrogator Eskell.* Even with Oliver, he was only ever Ryland.

"Yes," Ryland said, his own voice as soft as Coop's. He didn't want to startle Coop, didn't want to break the spell. "Yes, it's me. I'm here."

"They ... they put something in me." A trembling hand brushed the place behind his left ear, where the chip lay dead and inert. "I felt them do it."

He had been awake for the procedure? Ryland's gorge rose. "It's gone now." Or at least fried beyond repair.

"I don't remember anything after that." Coop raised his head. The red starbursts in his eyes stood out like wounds as his gaze searched Ryland's. "I was ... one of *them*, wasn't I? A chipped worker."

Ryland, not trusting himself to speak, only nodded.

"Before they put the chip in, they ... they took me to one of those rooms. Like the one I was in when I woke up with you. They ... they asked me questions."

Coop had been in the facility. Maybe while Ryland had been interrogating other prisoners. He should have known that was a likely possibility, of course. But he hadn't let himself think about it.

"It's over now," Ryland said uselessly. He reached out a hand to pat Coop's shoulder, and pulled it back just in time. He didn't have it in him to feel Coop flinch under his touch again.

A little clarity came into Coop's gaze. His eyes were bright and accusing. "When they brought me to that room ... I was afraid it would be *you.*"

"It wasn't," Ryland assured him. How clearly did Coop remember his interrogation? Did he know Ryland hadn't been a part of it, that Ryland hadn't even known he was arrested until it was too late?

"But it could have been." Coop's red-streaked eyes held his. Ryland fought the urge to look away.

"I wouldn't have done it," Ryland said. "I would have ... " His voice trailed off, because what would he have done? What *could* he have done? Condemned them both to certain death by trying to escape the building with him?

Only ... he had done it now, two years later. And they weren't dead. Maybe he could have done it then. If he had tried.

"I never gave you up," said Coop. "In the interrogation. I didn't give them your name. I didn't tell them about ... about us. About our plans." He gave the word *plans* a bitter twist, so faint it would have been undetectable to anyone who didn't know him as well as Ryland did.

Coop had never really believed those plans existed.

"Thank you," Ryland said. The words seemed inadequate. He knew – better than anyone – what an interrogation looked like. He knew the futility of trying to hold any information back. But Coop had. He had protected Ryland, even after he must have figured out that Ryland wasn't coming to his rescue.

He reached a hesitant hand out toward Coop. Coop drew away, pressing himself against the arm of the couch. Ryland brought his hand back to his lap.

"You kept me going, you know," Coop's voice was still raspy – from the screaming, Ryland thought. Those small tremors still ran through his body, shaking the cushion underneath them both. "Imagining us. Together. What we could have had. What you could still have. I imagined you running, once you figured out what had happened to me. Going to that cabin. Being free." He paused. His gaze cooled the tiniest bit. "If there ever was a cabin."

"There was," said Ryland. "There is."

"But you're still here," said Coop. "I thought ... when you didn't come, I thought you had run. I was glad for it. I was glad at least one of us would get to leave all this behind. But ... you're still *here*." As he repeated the words, Ryland knew he didn't mean this luxurious house. He meant the facility, and all that came with it.

"There was no point in going without you," said Ryland.

"Weren't you afraid I would tell them everything?"

Ryland had done his best not to think about it, just like with everything else about Coop's arrest. But yes, some part of him had foreseen that outcome. Some part of him had assumed it was inevitable.

"There was no point," Ryland repeated, "without you."

"So you just ... went on interrogating rebels. Went on doing to them what your friends were doing to me." A larger shudder ran through him. He clutched the side of his chest, where the broken rib was.

"Let me get you some ice for that."

"When you were interrogating my friends," said Coop, "with me right there in the next room ... did you ever think about how it could have been me?"

Yes. Yes, he had, that day and every day after. Every day for the past three years.

He opened his mouth. But the words caught in his throat.

What right did he have to complain about the past three years, after all? What right did he have to whine about his haunting? While he had been plagued by his ghosts, Coop had been dead, or the closest thing to it.

"They won't catch you again," Ryland promised. "I still own that cabin – or my other identity does. I'll get you there."

A mask of bitter resignation came across Coop's pain-pale face. "I've heard that before."

"I've risked my life more than once for you over the past two days," Ryland said. "If I was going to back out, I would have by now." He held his hand out to Coop again, palm up, like an offering. "I'll get you to that cabin."

Coop dropped his gaze to Ryland's hand. Ryland, practiced though he was at reading prisoners, couldn't tell what Coop was thinking.

At last, Coop placed a trembling hand in his. His skin was cold and clammy. He felt like ... well, like a man who had been dead less than an hour ago.

Ryland squeezed his hand. Coop squeezed back. The tiny, trembly gesture filled his heart more than any number of kisses could have back when they were together. The memory of Coop's empty face was still fresh in his mind.

"And you?" Coop asked.

Ryland frowned. "And me, what?"

"You said you'd get me to the cabin. What about you? Will you be there?"

Ryland's hand tensed in Coop's grip. He didn't even consciously realize it until Coop pulled away. He looked down at his now-empty palm, and regretted his instinctual response too late.

"That depends on you," Ryland said. "You've only just gotten free of the chip. I don't know where things stand between us – and you probably don't know, either. I don't want to assume anything. If you don't want me there, I'll understand."

"Do *you* want to be there?" Coop's eyes didn't release his. "Because you never seemed to want it before."

"Of course I do. I never stopped thinking about you, you know. Not for three years."

"If it's what you wanted," asked Coop, "then why aren't you there right now? Why aren't we both there?"

"It wasn't – "

"The right time. I know." Like his bloodshot gaze, Coop's small sigh felt like an accusation.

"What I want isn't what's important right now," said Ryland. "You should take some time to think. After you've had something to eat and a good night's sleep. You might not want to be with me, after everything." After Coop had gotten an up-close view of what Ryland's job entailed. After Coop had sat in a cell, waiting for a rescue that had never come.

Coop's gaze softened just enough to melt some of the tension from Ryland's shoulders. "I don't know much right now," he said. "I'm not even sure I know who I am anymore." His hand went to his head again. "But I do know I still want you. I want *us*." The ghost of a smile flickered across his strained face. "I know it's a boneheaded choice, one I shouldn't be making now and shouldn't have made back then. But just like back then, I also know I wouldn't be happy with any other choice than this."

Coop's words melted something in Ryland that had been frozen for three years. Something that had kept him on his feet all this time, clocking in to work, going through the motions.

Now he was left abruptly unsteady, like there was nothing holding him up. Like he was teetering on the edge of a cliff.

"I'll get you out of here first thing tomorrow morning," Ryland said. "After you've gotten some sleep. I wish I could give you longer to adjust, but they're searching for you. I'll join you as soon as I can."

Coop frowned. "Wouldn't it be safer for you if you came with me right away?"

Ryland's shaky footing grew more precarious. The abyss yawned open before him. "I should stay and keep an eye on the investigation, make sure your tracks are covered. Once I'm sure you're safe, I'll join you."

Coop's bloody gaze hardened.

"This isn't about covering my tracks and keeping me safe. You're not ready. Even now."

"You don't know what kind of hornets' nest I kicked over when I got you out. I need to make sure you're safe. If it's between risking your life by not keeping an eye on things here, or risking my own by staying behind too long, I know which choice I'd rather live with."

Coop shook his head. "No more excuses, Ry. Not *now*, after all this. Either you're coming with me, or you're not. Choose, Ry. Now."

Even though Coop was still trembling, his voice was steel. Ryland knew he meant what he said. Either Ryland ran away with him now, or he would never see him again.

And maybe that would be for the best. Coop didn't need Ryland in his life, a reminder of everything he had been through. Ryland could do Coop more good here, where he could watch the investigation, where he could make sure no one tracked Coop down.

Where Ryland wouldn't have to take that final step.

He stared down at the yawning abyss – and leapt.

"I'm coming with you," he said.

10

So many little luxuries. Ryland's house was stuffed with them. So many, and yet he struggled to fill the single duffel bag he had pulled out to pack for their departure.

What use would his espresso machine be on the run? And he could hardly pick up that expensive carpet and tuck it into his bag. The paintings on the walls ... even if they could have fit, none of them were worth bringing. They had come with the house; Ryland had never bothered changing them out.

Coop was still sleeping. Ryland wanted him to sleep as long as possible – although that wouldn't be much longer, since he wanted to leave before anyone would expect him at work. Ryland hadn't slept. His head had been too full of the plan they had settled on before he had made Coop go to bed for the night. Besides, the couch might look nice, but as a bed, it left a lot to be desired.

The metronome of Coop's breathing settled Ryland's heart as he crept into the bedroom and opened the dresser. As silently as he could, he slid open the drawers, one by one.

He stared down at the contents. What use would he have for his work suits where he was going? He tossed in a couple of pairs of socks and underwear, then peered into the drawers like a crystal ball, trying to find something worth bringing into his new life.

The metronome lost its rhythm. The bed shifted and groaned as Coop stirred. He gave a sleepy whimper of pain.

"Careful with that rib," Ryland warned. He turned around to see Coop wince as he struggled to a seated position. "Did I wake you?"

Coop shook his head. "Nightmare." His eyes went to the bag and the open drawers. "What are you doing?"

"Packing. Or trying to." Ryland grabbed a shirt and pair of pants at random and stuffed them into the bag. "You'll be arriving at the cabin empty-handed, I'm afraid. I don't have anything in your size, and buying things for you ahead of time would raise suspicions. If it's any consolation, I won't be much better off." Ryland zipped up the half-full bag.

"That's okay," said Coop. "I lost everything I owned three years ago." He bit his lip. Then he offered Ryland a tentative smile. "I have my freedom. And I have you. That's all I really need."

"How are you feeling?" Ryland asked, frowning as Coop winced again on his way out of bed.

"I could use some more of those painkillers." Coop wobbled on his feet. He grabbed at the wall to steady himself. "It's not just the rib, either. I hurt *everywhere.* And the burn cream helped last night, but the burns are hurting again."

Coop's electrode burns were the worst Ryland had ever seen, and no wonder. "I'll get you more burn cream." Ryland swallowed down a surge of guilt. He'd had to do it. That didn't make the memory of Coop's screams hurt any less. "But you're feeling well enough to go?"

Coop rubbed at the side of his chest with the broken rib. "I don't have much choice, do I?"

Unable to argue with that, Ryland hurried to the bathroom, where he grabbed two more pills for Coop. Over-the-counter – it was all he had. He also took the tube of burn cream. After a thought, he turned back and grabbed the whole bottle of pills. Coop would need it for the drive ahead of them.

He brought the pills to Coop, plus a glass of water. Coop swallowed them gratefully and lifted his shirt to spread the thick cream over the burns. "So," he said, "are we doing this?"

Ryland looked down at the duffel bag. He swept his gaze around the room, taking in the sight of everything he owned, and marveled at how little he cared that he would never see any of it again. "I guess we are," he said.

The blinding grin Coop managed through the pain made all Ryland's doubts disappear for a second. He could have left even the meager contents of the duffel bag behind and been content just to know Coop would be there to smile at him like that again.

In the garage, Ryland tossed the bag into the trunk of his car. Then, with a grimace, he fingered the blanket he had put back there last night. "Do you remember the plan?" What he was really asking was if Coop was still ready to go through with it.

"I hide in the trunk, under the blanket, until we get to Anderson Farm." The farm was the closest source of fresh vegetables, and did a brisk business this time of year. It was a logical enough place for Ryland to drive, even though it meant going well out of his way. It was also in a lightly surveilled area, and had a junkyard out back full of cars in various states of disrepair. It would be an easy enough place to do the handoff.

"My contact will meet us there." Ryland picked up where Coop had left off. "He'll take the car and junk it. We'll give him the cash and take the new car he brings for us." Ryland's contact had been surprised to hear from him after three years. But apparently his underground operation was still in business. He'd had no problem making the plans on short notice, so long as Ryland agreed to pay a rush fee.

"It's almost an hour to the farm," Ryland warned. "You won't be very comfortable back there. Especially with that rib."

"I'll be less comfortable if they catch me," Coop pointed out.

Again, Ryland couldn't argue. "After that, it's another ten hours to the cabin. You should be able to ride in front for most of that time, but you'll have to get in the trunk again if we see anything suspicious." Had they set up checkpoints yet? If so, Ryland would be in just as much danger of being recognized as

Coop. Above suspicion or not, it would be hard to explain what he was doing several hours away from the facility, and in a car he didn't own. But he didn't bring that up with Coop. This was still the best chance they had.

"I can manage," Coop said, although he rubbed his chest again at the thought. He paused. "You know, as much as you told me about that cabin, I was never sure it was real."

"It's real," Ryland promised. "It's got a working wood stove in the living room, and a hiking trail out back that leads to the lake, and a fenced yard for a dog. And a mouse problem, last I heard. Sorry about that."

"I've always wanted a dog," Coop said. "One of those wiener dogs with the stubby legs. You know, I'm not entirely sure I didn't stay dead in that interrogation room. This is all too good to be true."

"Let's not count any chickens. We still have to make it there first." He climbed into the driver's seat. Coop swung one leg into the trunk.

Ryland's gut knotted. "Wait."

Coop froze as Ryland climbed back out of the car. "What is it?"

"Are you really sure you want this?"

Coop stared at him in disbelief, one leg still hoisted up awkwardly. "What's the alternative, exactly?"

"I don't know." All Ryland knew was that the knot in his stomach had started *moving*, like a mass of squirming snakes. "We're moving pretty fast. Maybe we should slow down."

"You were the one who said we had to go right away," Coop pointed out.

"I know," said Ryland. "It's just … " He shook his head. "I don't know. Put your leg down – that's got to hurt."

Coop swung his leg back down. "It's just what? Still not the right time?"

Ryland winced at the bitterness in Coop's voice. "It's not like that."

"Then what is it?" His eyes searched Ryland's. "If this isn't what you want, you need to tell me now. I meant what I said last night – no more stringing me along. The answer is either yes or it's no."

"The answer is yes." But Ryland couldn't seem to take the two steps back to the driver's seat.

Coop shook his head. "I should have known."

"We're doing this. I just need a minute."

"You had *months.* The past three years would never have happened if you'd made your choice a little quicker – did you ever think about that?"

"Every day," Ryland said tightly. "But what do you want me to do about it now?"

Coop lowered his head, releasing Ryland's gaze. It didn't feel like a reprieve.

"If it wasn't for me," Coop said quietly, "you would never even consider leaving, would you?"

Ryland blinked. "Why would I?"

"Maybe because you're tired of torturing people for a living."

"Do you really want to go there now?"

"Even when you were planning on running away with me before," said Coop, "you never had a problem with your job. It was only ever about me."

"Again, is this really the time? We've had this fight. It never ends anywhere good."

"Why *not* do it now? We sure don't seem to be doing anything else. Like getting in the car and leaving."

"Someone has to do what I do," said Ryland. "I happen to be good at it. No matter how much you dislike both of those facts, it doesn't make either of them any less true."

Coop shook his head slowly. "Why be with me if you think I'm such a horrible criminal?"

"I could ask you the same question. If you hate me so much, why were you ever with me?"

"I used to ask myself that question all the time," said Coop.

Ryland's heart dropped into his shoes. He had thought Coop would say, *I don't hate you.*

Maybe Coop was right. Maybe this was the best time for this fight, after all. It would have happened eventually – two years together had made Ryland certain of that. At least now maybe

Coop would realize his mistake before they were stuck with each other.

Ryland started to revise the plan in his mind. He would drive Coop to the farm. They would make the handoff as planned. Coop would take the car on his own – it would be riskier, but not that much riskier. Ryland would pay his contact a bonus to make up for not leaving the car with him, and then –

"But I always knew the answer," Coop said, interrupting his thoughts. "Or I never would have stayed with you."

"Because I'm that good in bed?" Ryland's teasing tone fell flat.

Coop rolled his eyes. His lips twitched upward in the hint of a smile. "Because I love you, you bonehead."

"I love you too," Ryland said. "I never stopped. If I could do it again, I would have come for you." As he said the words, he realized he meant them.

Coop shook his head. "No sense feeling guilty about things you can't change. I just wish … " His words trailed off.

"You wish what?" Ryland pressed.

"I wish," Coop said softly, "you would recognize that loving me – just that alone – is a rebellion against the system you serve. I wish you could admit to yourself that you don't support everything you work for as much as you think you do."

Anger rose in Ryland's belly – the familiar anger of so many fights, so much retreaded ground. He opened his mouth to argue.

Then he shook his head. "There'll be plenty of time to fight later," he said, answering Coop's hint of a smile with one of his own. "At the cabin. For now, we need to go." He watched Coop tensely, waiting to see whether the other man would accept his offer of a truce.

"Then ... we're doing this?"

"We're doing this." *If you still want to do this*, he silently added. *If you still want me.* "Get in that trunk."

"Gladly," Coop said as he swung his leg up again.

Then both of them froze at the sound of sirens.

They looked at each other. Then toward the road, where the sirens were growing louder.

"It's probably not us," Coop said with a tremor in his voice.

"Probably not," Ryland agreed. "But let's get moving anyway."

Ryland hadn't even closed the driver's-side door when he heard the screech of tires from beyond the garage door. Outside the door, flashing lights strobed.

I'm sorry, Coop.

11

— · —

In all the years he had worked at the facility, Ryland had never realized the walls of the cells slanted inward slightly, giving them the impression of being constantly about to collapse atop a prisoner's head. Or maybe Ryland's mind was playing tricks on him. Maybe he was losing it already, even though he had only been sitting in the bare concrete cell for a few hours. Or *had* it been a few hours? Maybe it had been less than one hour. Maybe it had been days.

The cell had a faint musty odor, like an old basement after a rainstorm. Something else Ryland had never noticed before. He'd have to bring it up with the maintenance staff at some point, see if water was getting in somewhere.

As if he'd ever have a chance to make a suggestion to the maintenance staff again. He laughed – and jumped as the sound echoed off the close walls.

The short, sharp burst of laughter woke the painful spots in his chest. He rubbed the bruises gently, wincing each time his fingers hit an especially tender place. They hadn't been gentle with him when they had brought him in. That was the flipside of being above suspicion – when they had found out they were wrong about him, they had taken it personally.

The cell door began to swing inward with a near-silent swish. He sprang to his feet, then winced as the movement showed him still more bruises he didn't know he had. He took an involuntary step back.

He didn't want to show fear. He didn't want to be like those prisoners who collapsed as soon as someone looked at them wrong. He had always thought of those types as pathetic, although on the bright side, they tended to be easy to interrogate.

But it was hard to keep his calm when he knew better than anyone what awaited him.

How long would it be before his own interrogation? Was that why they were here? To drag him off to one of those rooms where he had spent so much time?

But it was Oliver who stepped in. Ryland let out his breath in relief. "So you heard," he said, trying for a sheepish smile.

Oliver didn't return his smile. He looked Ryland up and down with pain in his eyes. "I didn't want it to be true."

"Believe me, I didn't want to be here either." Ryland stepped forward. "Coop. The chipped worker. Do you know where he is?"

As Ryland approached, Oliver took a step back, holding his hands in front of his chest as if to ward him away. The pain in his eyes flared; his lip curled in disgust. "You really do care more about him than about all the rest of us, don't you? You turned traitor for a nice piece of ass. I can't believe it."

Ryland bristled at the description of Coop. "It's not like that." But wasn't it? He had made his choice. He had chosen Coop.

It had been so hard for him to take that final leap. But now that he had, he couldn't find it in him to regret the choice. Even here. Even now.

"I hoped I was wrong," Oliver said. "I hoped they wouldn't find anything. I was *sure* they wouldn't find anything, and I'd have to apologize for doubting you. I was going to grovel. Buy you an expensive dinner. The works."

Ryland frowned, trying to make sense of Oliver's words. He couldn't be saying ... he couldn't mean *he* had ...

"You did this?" He whispered the words, not wanting to lend them legitimacy by speaking them too loudly.

But Oliver's eyes only grew more distant, his disgusted lips a thin white line. "*You* did this. All I did was pass on the information that you and the chipped worker had a history."

"You did this." The one person he had known he could trust with his secrets. The one person he had counted as a friend. "How could you?"

"*You're* angry?" Oliver gave his head a sharp shake. "I'm the only one here with a right to be angry. You're just facing the consequences of your actions. What exactly did you think was going to happen when you breached the security of your own facility and ran off with government property?"

"He's not ... " Ryland looked down at his hands, which had clenched into tight and painful fists. He slowly released his fingers. His nails left half-moon marks along his palms. "Where is he?"

"He's back where he belongs." Oliver's voice was clipped, cold. The kind of voice Ryland imagined he must use with his prisoners. "The chipped-worker trial will continue, with or without you. There's no reason your stupidity should ruin it for everyone else. If this works out, we'll all have chipped workers as assistants one day."

"Back where he belongs," Ryland repeated slowly. He was afraid to think about what that might mean. "You mean with the technology division, or ... " Would they try to put a replacement chip in him? Could they even do that? Ryland wanted to be sick. It would have been better for Coop – better for both of them – if he had died in that interrogation room.

"Back here," Oliver said impatiently. "In the facility. Weren't you listening? I said the trial isn't over. He's been assigned to me now – and he's proved himself to be quite a helpful assistant so far." He shook his head slowly. "Although I have to say, I don't see the appeal. He can't have been all that attractive even back when he still had a will of his own."

Oliver thought Coop was still chipped.

Oliver thought Coop was still chipped.

How? The difference between Coop with the chip active and Coop as himself had been so stark – how could they not have known the difference? Unless ... unless Coop had thought fast enough, and put on a convincing enough act, to make his captors believe he was still under the chip's influence.

And if they didn't know he had his own will back ... he still had a chance to escape.

Ryland's breath caught. He sagged sideways against the wall.

Coop could still escape.

Oliver made a disgusted noise deep in his throat. "You're not going to cry for him, are you? Because I don't think I can stand to stick around for that. My stomach can't take it."

His words were cruel, but pain flared in his eyes again as he spoke. Ryland remembered their last dinner together, how eager Oliver had been for Ryland to put the memory of Coop behind him. How eager for Ryland to come to his apartment and share a quiet evening and a special bottle.

"I know this isn't what you expected of me," he said. "I know you're hurt, and I don't know if I can ever make that up to you." His eyes searched Oliver's in a silent plea. "But if our friendship ever meant anything to you ... if *I* ever meant anything to you ... help him. Please. Help him get out of here."

Oliver's face contorted. "I thought you might ask me to save you. I thought it might even be hard to say no. But you're asking me to save *him*? Really?"

"It's the last favor I'll ever ask you." The last favor he would ever be *able* to ask him. "And there are plenty of chipped workers to take his place. What does it matter to you which one is here?"

And how many of those chipped workers had been ripped away from people they loved? How many of them still haunted the people who had lost them? But Ryland wouldn't think about that. He had never wanted to think about that. Bad enough that he had loved a rebel. Bad enough that he had lost him.

He wasn't going to turn rebel. No matter what Coop thought.

But then, what did it matter now, anyway? He was dead no matter what.

If he was lucky. If they didn't do to him what they had done to Coop.

"I'm no traitor," said Oliver. "Unlike you, apparently. And it's not like it matters to *him* where he is. He's chipped – he doesn't know the difference." He looked briefly queasy. "What exactly did you order him to do when you took him home? Did you go to bed with him for old time's sake? Did you tell him to do all the things he used to do, and say all the things he used to say? Did he obey your orders?"

A full-body flinch ran through Ryland. "Don't," he said tightly.

"You're the one who took your chipped ex-lover home with you. What else am I supposed to think?" He shook his head. "I can't believe I ever ... " He didn't finish the sentence.

Ryland knew there was no point in pushing further. And yet he tried anyway, because what did he have to lose? "At least let me see him. Just one more time."

"I can't do this anymore. I can't listen to this." Oliver turned away. "Goodbye, Ryland."

With his hand on the doorknob, he looked over his shoulder. "It'll be about time for your interrogation to start soon, anyway. I won't be handling that. *I* know better than to ignore a conflict of interest." For a second, Oliver looked like he was about to cry. "I hope you resist for a good long time. I hope it hurts."

Then he was gone.

12

As the next shock hit Ryland, his lungs contracted, stealing his breath so he couldn't even scream. Fire raced through him as if someone had set his veins alight from the inside. His back arched, his muscles tightening, his limbs twitching without him willing it. His body was no longer under his control. He hung suspended in the pain, unable to imagine a time before it or a time after.

And all he could think was, *This is what Coop felt.*

The pain stopped as quickly as it had started. The interrogator stared down at him with arms crossed. "The names of your resistance contacts," he said again.

Ryland shook his head weakly, the movement sending sharp spikes of pain down his exhausted muscles. "I told you," he gasped, still struggling to regain his breath. "I'm not ... working for the resistance."

The interrogator was a newbie. Of course he was – they'd had to assign Ryland to the new guy, because he was the only one in the facility Ryland didn't have at least a passing relationship with. This junior interrogator had only been at the facility for a few weeks. Ryland wasn't even sure he remembered his name. Black? Blake? Not like it mattered to Ryland. He would just as soon call the man Interrogator Asshole.

Unfortunately for Ryland, he was the type of newbie to follow the rules to the letter, not the type who made sloppy mistakes. He hadn't taken his eyes off Ryland for a second, nor had he given Ryland an opening to attack when he had transferred him from the handcuffs to the chair's restraints. It figured that *now* was when the facility would start hiring new interrogators who were competent from the start. They couldn't have done that a couple of years ago, when Ryland had drawn the short straw and been assigned to train a bunch of –

Another shock obliterated Ryland's thoughts. A part of him watched detachedly as his body convulsed against the chair. It was funny, really – all the times he had done this to his prisoners, and he had never really known how it felt. Sure, he had imagined it, but imagination didn't come close to the real thing. Imagination couldn't capture the feeling of one's own bones being set aflame.

Coop had gone through this three years ago, and he hadn't given Ryland up.

The shock stopped, releasing him. His head flopped heavily to his chest. He couldn't seem to lift his neck, and couldn't imagine why it would be worth the effort.

Where was Coop now?

Ryland hoped he had made his escape already. That he had made it to the handoff, and found a way to pay Ryland's contact. That he would make it to the cabin. The cabin had always mattered to him more than to Ryland, anyway.

He hadn't understood, before, how the thought of him escaping alone had been enough to sustain Coop. He hadn't understood how Coop had felt anything other than bitterness once he had known Ryland wasn't coming for him. Now he got it.

The interrogator was talking again. "How long have you been working with the resistance?"

"I ... told you," Ryland said without lifting his head. "I'm not ... working with them. I never have."

"What information have you been passing to them?" The interrogator's heavy footsteps echoed off the walls. When Ryland looked up from under his lashes, the interrogator had walked back to the controls, his hand on the dial. He turned it up a notch. Ryland let out a pathetic little whimper.

But the interrogator didn't press the button. Not yet. "You know how this ends," he said. "You know it better than anyone. So why not spare yourself the pain?" Under his stone exterior, he sounded truly baffled.

"Because I'm telling you the truth," said Ryland. "It was never about their cause." He ignored a stab of guilt as, in his mind, he saw Coop's reproachful face. "It was only ever about

Coop." And that had never been enough for Coop. But that hardly mattered now.

"Cooper Byrd," the interrogator said. "According to the information Oliver Marotti provided, the two of you were sexually and romantically involved for two years. You were fully aware of his resistance activities for the entire time. And yet you continued the relationship. You didn't report Mr. Byrd's criminal activity. Mr. Marotti suspects you may have actively worked to cover up his activities on at least one occasion."

Had Oliver's jealousy poisoned their friendship so thoroughly? Or was he truly so loyal that he was willing to sacrifice all other loyalties? "That's my worst crime," said Ryland. "Not turning in a known rebel. If you want to lock me up for that, fine. Do what you want with me. But I don't have any other information to give you."

"If you didn't have at least some sympathy for his cause," the interrogator insisted, "you would have turned him in."

With an effort, Ryland lifted his head. "You've never known anyone to do something stupid for love before?"

"What information have you passed to the resistance?" the interrogator asked without replying. "What are the names of your contacts?" His face was stone. He looked like he had no personal experience with love and its accompanying stupidity.

Instead of arguing, Ryland threw back his head and laughed.

After all, it was hilarious, really. He of all people knew how futile it was to hold back information during an interrogation.

He of all people knew everyone talked eventually. If he'd actually had any of the information the interrogator wanted, he would have coughed it up in a heartbeat. But he had nothing to give. And because of that, he would suffer the same fate as the most stubbornly defiant prisoners.

Well. He did have *one* thing he could give up. Coop's chip wasn't working anymore. Coop was free, and they didn't know it.

But he was damned if he would ever tell him *that*.

Which, he supposed, made him every bit as stupid as those stubborn prisoners, after all.

When the next shock came, it ripped through him like an inferno. The pain engulfed him, worse than before, worse than anyone could survive. He was going to die right here and now – how could he not? From a far distance, he heard himself scream. His screams didn't sound like anything human.

But this was still better than what Coop had felt, after Ryland had sat him down unsuspecting in one of these chairs to short out the chip. Coop had endured it, and so could Ryland.

And if it killed him, like it had Coop …

Well, at least then the pain would stop, and Coop's secret would be safe.

He could only hope they wouldn't be able to bring him back.

"Coop," he whispered on a ragged breath as the pain faded.

The interrogator's stone mask briefly broke as his face twisted in disgust. "I heard all the stories about you, you know," he said.

"The prisoners you broke that everyone thought would never talk. The one rebel you had confessing everything in less than five minutes. I looked up to you. I wanted to *be* you."

His hand crept back toward the button. Ryland braced himself for the pain.

The door opened.

The interrogator looked over his shoulder, annoyance crossing his face. "I'm in the middle of an interrogation," he snapped. "What do you – "

His voice cut off as the blood drained from his face.

Coop stood in the doorway, a gun in his hand. Blood dotted his shirt and freckled his face. His eyes were set in a determined stare that left no room for fear.

Ryland's whisper had summoned an avenging angel.

"Your interrogation is over," Coop said, and he pulled the trigger.

13

The walls of the hallway closed in, seeming to grow narrower and narrower. Ryland's hurried footsteps and Coop's echoed through the close space – as behind them, the echoes of their pursuers grew ever louder.

Ryland's steps faltered. Under the sterile tang of the facility, he smelled his own sweat. He smelled like a prisoner. He smelled like fear.

His steps faltered. Coop pulled ahead, and shot a tight-lipped look over his shoulder. "Keep going," Coop warned, puffing out the words between breaths. "Don't slow down."

"Stop!" someone shouted behind him.

Ryland's fingers tightened around the gun he had stolen from the interrogator. He spun to face his pursuers. Two guards advanced on him, weapons in hand. He knew their faces, although he couldn't place their names. They were often on duty when he was working; they regularly exchanged nods on busy days, and a few words about the weather when things were slower.

He started to raise the stolen gun. His hand shook. This wasn't like being in an interrogation room with a prisoner. In an interrogation, he didn't hear his heartbeat thundering in his ears. He didn't sense his own impending death with every indrawn breath.

He was too slow. The guards' weapons came up first. His heart gave a shuddering beat as he lowered his head in resignation. It was too late. The best he could hope for was that they would shoot him before –

Two gunshots, one after the other. Ryland squeezed his eyes shut instinctively. A high-pitched ringing in his ears replaced the drumbeat of his heart.

When he opened his eyes again, the guards were lying on the ground in front of him, a pool of red spreading around them. Neither of them moved to get up.

Coop lowered his gun. "Come on. There'll be more where that came from." His voice was perfectly steady. Without another word, he turned and started running again.

With one last look at the fallen guards, Ryland took off after him.

"This way," he said, motioning Coop down a hallway to the left. His voice was faint and shaky. He could barely hear himself over the persistent ringing in his ears. "The stairwell leads to a tunnel. It comes out – "

"A block away, by the drugstore," Coop finished for him. "The resistance *does* know a few things about this place, you know." As he followed Ryland through the stairwell door, he shot Ryland a sideways look. "I didn't think you, of all people, would freeze under fire." Then he shot Ryland a brief smile. "No offense meant."

"And I didn't think ... you were so good ... with a gun," Ryland puffed as he ran down the stairs, feeling every bit of the strain the electric shocks had put on his body.

Coop shot him a heart-stopping grin over his shoulder. "Look at that. We can still surprise each other."

At the bottom of the stairs was a metal door with a keypad next to it. Ryland typed in the code and held his breath. The door clicked open. They hadn't changed all the codes yet. Sloppy of them.

The door closed behind them. Dim yellow emergency lighting lit the tunnel, reminding Ryland of the facility at night. The walls curved upward into a sloped concrete ceiling. The musty smell of the cell was even stronger down here.

Ryland wanted nothing more than to sag against the wall until he stopped shaking. He forced himself to keep going. But he let himself slow to a jog.

Coop shot him a worried look. "Hey, you okay?"

Ryland tried to smile. "In the past few hours, I've been arrested, beat up, shocked repeatedly, and shot at. That's a lot of new experiences all at once."

Coop reached for Ryland's hand. He squeezed it. "It's okay now," he said. "We're going to be okay."

"There are guards at the exit," Ryland warned.

"And we'll deal with them when we get there." Coop gave his hand another rhythmic squeeze, like he was showing Ryland's heart how to beat properly again. "One step after another, okay? Focus on my voice."

"Do I really look that bad?"

"You're pretty pale. Pale enough that I hope you're not going to pass out on me. I may be your hero tonight, but my super-powers don't extend to carrying you out of here."

"You've done more than enough already," Ryland assured him. He shot Coop a look. "How did you do it?"

Coop shrugged without breaking his stride. "They thought I was still chipped. It was easy enough to catch that jerk of an interrogator off guard."

Ryland bit his lip shut on the impulse to defend Oliver. "Is he dead?"

Coop must have caught something in his tone, because he frowned. "Friend of yours?"

"Not anymore." Ryland tried to put the memory of Oliver's hurt, disgusted face out of his mind. "Still ... the element of surprise can only get you so far. How did you overpower him without a weapon? How did you get down to the interrogation level without being caught? How did you get the key to the interrogation room where I ... "

His voice trailed off. Because, of course, he knew the answers to all of those questions. He had never asked Coop about the specifics of his work for the resistance, just like Coop had never asked for the specifics of Ryland's work. It had been just one more of those things Ryland had preferred not to think about. But now he thought he had a good idea of what that work had involved. This wasn't Coop's first infiltration of a secure facility.

The silent look Coop shot him confirmed Ryland's suspicions.

Coop's steps faltered. He steadied himself against the wall, wrapping his other hand around his broken rib. Ryland paused, frowning. "Hey. You okay?"

Coop tried for a smile. "Still better than you."

"You shouldn't be running like that with a broken rib. Not to mention ... everything else." Like the fact that only a day ago, Ryland had killed him. "I don't know how you kept up that pace for so long."

"Adrenaline." Coop shot Ryland a pale smile. "It's a wonder drug."

"Well, you can't keep going like that much longer. You'll collapse."

"No choice. I'm getting you out of here."

Ryland frowned as he caught a glint of red on Coop's fingers. Coop wasn't holding the broken rib, after all, but a spot slightly lower down. Red oozed onto his hand and soaked through his shirt, spreading slowly but steadily. Ryland hadn't known any of the blood on his shirt was his own.

"What happened?" he asked, trying and failing to keep the alarm out of his voice.

"Your friend fought back. It's nothing serious. I'll take care of it once we're out of here."

"*I'll* take care of it," Ryland promised. "For now, slow down a bit, okay? Before I have to carry *you* out of here."

"No slowing down on a rescue mission." With another wan smile, Coop pushed himself off the wall. He returned to his jogging pace, looking for all the world like nothing was wrong. But he kept his hand clutched to his side.

They were getting close to the exit. Ryland placed a finger to his lips as he slowed his steps, sacrificing speed for quiet. Coop nodded and matched his pace to Ryland's.

They crept the last few feet to the door. Ryland lifted a finger to the keypad, then paused, shooting Coop a questioning look. Coop nodded. He pulled out his gun.

Ryland's chest constricted as he tapped in the code. As soon as the lock clicked, he swung the door open. The guards spun to face them, surprise turning to alarm on their faces –

Two more shots. They fell together, each of them with a neat hole through the forehead. Ryland stared at Coop. How had he never known how *scary* his gentle and easygoing lover was?

Up and down the sidewalk, under the glow of the street-lamps, startled heads turned at the gunshots. "Run," Coop ordered – and then took his own advice, pushing his beleaguered body harder than should have been possible.

Given that Coop was both bleeding and recently brought back from the dead, Ryland could hardly complain about his own comparatively minor aches and pains. He matched Coop's pace. He felt the night closing in around them as tightly as the hallways had a few moments ago. Trapping them.

"Where to now?" he asked, trying not to sound as despairing as he felt. Sure, they were free, but for how long? They had nowhere to go. His house was out of the question. His car was probably evidence by now. He searched for other ideas, and came up blank. This wasn't his area of expertise. He belonged in an interrogation room, not out in the field.

"Steal a car," Coop said immediately, pausing beside a sad rusted-out specimen. "Whoever owns this hunk of junk won't be shelling out for the extra security package – if it's even available on something this old. No one will be able to track us. Shoe." With the last word, he motioned toward Ryland's shoes.

With no time to ask why, Ryland pulled off a shoe and handed it to Coop. Coop started to swing it at the back window, then stopped with a wince, clutching his chest. He handed the shoe back to Ryland.

Ryland slammed it into the back window as hard as he could. After three tries, the window shattered. Coop reached in and forward to unlock the driver's side door.

Coop slid into the driver's seat with a grunt of pain. He bent with a sharp whimper and fiddled around under the steering column. Ryland watched with a frown, trying to keep one eye on Coop and another on their surroundings. "Are you trying to hotwire the car? I don't think that actually – "

The sudden roar of the engine cut off his words. Coop climbed into the passenger seat, motioning Ryland to the side he had abandoned. "I think … " he said, his voice wan all of a sudden. "I think you should drive."

Ryland frowned at the thick smear of blood across the seat. "We need to look at that wound."

"Not now," Coop said tightly. "Drive!"

Ryland peeled away from the curb. He shot a worried look at Coop, who was hunched over in his seat, clutching his side with both hands now.

"Don't worry about the car," Coop said. "If you're feeling guilty, you can get his address from the registration, mail him a few hundred bucks. This thing can't be worth much more than that."

"It's not the car I'm worried about," Ryland said as he tore through every red light he saw.

"Just drive," said Coop. "Get us to that farm."

Ryland made it onto the highway, where he slowed his frantic pace, letting himself blend into the anonymity of rush-hour traffic. "I doubt my contact will still be waiting," he warned.

"You can get in touch with him when you're there," Coop said. His voice was still impossibly steady. Maybe it just hadn't hit him yet – how close they had both come to death.

Ryland wasn't sure it had hit *him* yet. He had come within inches of ending up dead in that interrogation room. Or worse, with a chip in his head. And then the guards in the hallway – and at the end of the tunnel ... by all rights, he should have been dead by now.

He should have been dead.

The same detachment he had felt in the interrogation room came over him as he watched his hands begin to tremble on the steering wheel. He tightened his grip until his fingers turned white and his fingertips went numb.

"Keep driving," Coop said, his voice soft and hypnotic. "It's okay. You're okay."

The gunshots echoed in Ryland's ears. His vision narrowed to a tight, dim tunnel. "Maybe you should drive."

"I don't think that's such a good idea."

Something in Coop's tone made Ryland look at him sharply. He drew in his breath. Coop's shirt glistened with wet blood. It spilled out around his fingers and wet the seat underneath him.

"We need to deal with that wound *now*." Ryland started to pull onto the shoulder.

Coop shook his head. He grabbed the wheel with a blood-slick hand and jerked it back to the left. "Don't slow down," he ordered. "Keep going. This is your only chance at freedom." He flashed Ryland a faint smile. His lips were so pale. "No slowing down on a rescue mission, remember?"

Ryland didn't smile back. "*Our* only chance at freedom," he corrected. His eyes returned to the blood leaking out of Coop. So much blood.

Coop leaned his head back. He closed his eyes. "I'm glad I was able to get you out."

"You shouldn't have pushed yourself so hard." If he hadn't run like that – shot like that – if he had slowed down to do something about that wound –

"We would both have gotten caught." Coop's voice grew choppy as his breathing turned ragged. "Better this way. For both of us."

"You shouldn't have come back for me." The road ahead of him was blurry all of a sudden. "You should have saved yourself."

"You will be free," Coop said. "You'll be out of ... that place. That's all I really wanted." His head sagged to one side.

Ryland swung the car onto the shoulder and slammed on the brakes. With trembling hands, he lifted Coop's shirt. A jagged knife wound gaped open under his ribs. The bleeding was finally slowing now. Too late.

"Coop," Ryland whispered, a fervent mantra, as he pressed his hands uselessly to the wound. "Coop. Coop."

In the interrogation room, his mantra had brought Coop back. He knew it wouldn't work this time.

"I love you," Coop whispered, and then he was gone.

14

The fish weren't biting. That was no surprise. From his spot at the end of the weathered dock, Ryland watched the sky turn from golden to orange-red. He had been out here since dawn, minus a break for lunch, with nothing to show for it but a sunburn across the bridge of his nose. Oh, and probably a few splinters in his ass.

As the temperature dropped, the breeze turned from refreshing to chilly. It carried the scent of someone's barbecue from across the lake. His stomach growled.

"All right, you wily little critters," he muttered to the fish he knew had to be laughing at him under the surface of the lake. "You win. Again." He started to reel his line in.

Then he felt a tug. Was that – could it be ... He reeled faster. The hook broke the surface, a small silver fish dangling from the end. Its scales caught the golden light as it flopped uselessly.

"Oh no you don't," said Ryland with a grin of triumph as he plucked the fish off the hook. It nearly slithered out of his hands – what right did fish have to be so *slippery*? – but he popped it into the bucket that, until now, had never held anything but rainwater. "Victory at last. I'm having fish for dinner tonight."

He whistled a tune under his breath as he walked the narrow trail through the woods that led back to the cabin. Old Mr. Reynolds, with his ridiculous silver mustache, was out walking that fat bulldog of his. Mr. Reynolds marked his cheery demeanor with a raise of his eyebrows. "You finally caught one, did you?"

Ryland tried to hide his sudden tension. He did his best to be invisible to his neighbors, but they had noticed his pathetic attempts at fishing. "You don't have to sound so surprised about it," he said easily. He gave the dog a scratch behind the ears before letting them pass.

"Well done, Brian," Mr. Reynolds said as he continued on his way. "I knew you had it in you."

It took Ryland a second or two to realize he wasn't talking to the dog. Even now, he still wasn't used to answering to his new name. Mr. Reynolds only knew him by the new name, of course. Just like everyone else around here. Ryland doubted he or anyone else would be too keen on celebrating his accomplishment if they knew who Ryland really was.

He didn't know Mr. Reynolds's politics – it wasn't the kind of thing you brought up when making small talk on the trail. But one of the reasons he had chosen this town, way back when he had been making plans for him and Coop, was that it was a low-level center of rebel activity. It was too small and sleepy a place for anyone to bother doing anything to shut down that activity – the country had bigger problems. But it was the kind of place where, if anyone were to find out Ryland was on the run, they wouldn't be quick to turn him in.

Not unless they knew what he had done *before* going on the run.

The trail led him to his back fence, which he had left un-latched. Inside the fence, the grass was trimmed ruthlessly short – Ryland had to do something to occupy his time, after all. His failed attempts at a garden lay brown and scraggly along the worn wood of the back wall.

Ryland turned the key in the back lock, gave the door a kick in the sticky spot, and swung it open. It squealed as it let him in. The familiar smell of the cabin, like smoke and old wood, greeted him. He kicked off his boots and set his fishing supplies by the door. He hurried for the kitchen, turning away from the fireplace Coop would have loved, the armchair where he could so easily imagine Coop curling up under a blanket with a book. His whistling ceased.

He set the bucket down on the kitchen counter with a slam. The fish had ceased its flopping, and now lay inert, staring up at him with one glassy eye.

"Now I've just got to figure out how to cook you for dinner," Ryland said, trying to keep up his cheerful tone. "I didn't go to all the trouble of catching you not to get something out of it." He stared into the fish's dead eye. It was going to stare at him when he cut its head off, wasn't it? And did fish bleed? He hoped not. His stomach flopped like the fish had when he had pulled it out of the water.

He shook his head at himself. Coop would have laughed at him for feeling squeamish about a fish, considering all the things he had done to his prisoners without the slightest hint of queasiness. That is, if Coop had been in the mood to laugh about Ryland's former profession. Would they have come to a point, eventually, where they could laugh about it?

Oh god. Coop.

Ryland's vision blurred. His chest constricted. He let out a small hiccup. Tears landed in the bucket with tiny plops, like a summer drizzle.

He was crying over a damn *fish*.

"Pull yourself together," he muttered to himself, swiping at his eyes with the back of his hand. He wasn't doing Coop any favors by getting all teary-eyed over nothing. He owed it to Coop to live a happy life here in the cabin that should have been Coop's. Happy enough for both of them.

It was what Coop would have wanted. He knew because it was all he had wanted for Coop, back when he had thought he was going to die in that interrogation room.

Coop shouldn't have come to rescue him. He should have run.

He swallowed hard and forced the tears down. He stared into the fish's eye, and tried to ignore the stinging in his own eyes. "Enough," he said. "We're moving on, you hear me? We're going to figure out how to cook you, and then I'm going to eat you for dinner. And you're going to be delicious."

And after that, he would light a fire as the temperature dropped and darkness crept in. He would curl up in the armchair he had chosen for Coop, and finally make progress on the book he had picked up at the library last week and hadn't yet been able to concentrate on. He would read until he was tired enough to sleep without nightmares. Then he would curl up under the quilt Coop would have loved, in a bed big enough for two, and sleep alone.

Alone. Just like every day he had spent here so far.

He was trying. He was trying so hard. Trying to get back into reading again, to learn to fish, to take up chess and woodcarving and half a dozen other aborted hobbies. He was trying to relax. He was trying to be happy.

He was trying for Coop.

And sometimes it worked. When the sun was up and the weather was good and he could empty his mind for a while. When he wasn't inside these four walls that were somehow filled with memories of Coop even though Coop had never set foot in here.

It wouldn't have been so bad if he'd had a purpose. Something to occupy his time. Retirement wasn't all it was cracked up to be, and not only because even his considerable savings were bound to run out eventually. And yet the thought of stepping back into an interrogation room made him sick. Not because he imagined himself in the chair, but because he imagined Coop there.

It was only now, too late, that he understood that was part of why it had taken him so long to fully commit to his decision. Some part of him must have known that if he ever admitted it was Coop he truly wanted, that he cared more about the rebel in his bed than he did about his job getting information out of people who were no different from Coop, he would never be able to go back. He had a yawning void where his professional self used to be, and he no longer knew what to fill it with. He only knew that he had killed that self when he had made his choice.

And yet he didn't regret the choice he had made. Even though it had all gone wrong.

All he regretted was the empty life it had led to.

"It wouldn't have been empty to Coop," Ryland said. "He would have loved all this. Even figuring out how to cut up a fish for dinner."

Ryland would have loved it too, if only he'd had Coop here to share it with.

"We're going to do this for him," Ryland informed the fish with grim determination. "We'll live the life he should have gotten. We'll *enjoy* this, dammit." He flopped the fish onto a cutting board and searched the knife block. What kind of knife was he supposed to use for a fish, anyway? All he knew was what to use on a prisoner. Maybe he should have asked Mr. Reynolds for advice.

You absolute bonehead. Coop's voice was as clear as if he had been standing beside Ryland in the kitchen that should have been his.

Ryland jumped. "Not again," he muttered. "You've got to stop doing this, brain. We're both lucky I wasn't holding a knife."

If you really want to live for me, said the imagined version of Coop in his head, undeterred, *you can do better than waiting around all day to catch a fish.*

"This is what you wanted," Ryland said, even as he shook his head at himself for answering his own brain out loud. "You wanted all this, and I can't give it to you, so I can do the next best thing and enjoy it." Who did he think he was going to convince, anyway? The fish?

But is it what you *want?* imaginary Coop asked, implacable.

"Of course not. What I want – what I've always wanted – is you."

And if you can't have me, what do you want?

It was the question he had avoided asking himself all this time, because he didn't know the answer. He wasn't sure there *was* an answer. All he knew was that he was restless out here. He missed working, even though the thought of the facility made him sick. He missed purpose. He missed not being alone.

"I can't go back to my work," Ryland said. He would be on the run for the rest of his life. But even if Norby would have taken him back with open arms, it wouldn't have made a difference.

His imagined version of Coop fell silent. But he saw Coop in his mind, looking at him with that familiar reproachful expression. When he blinked away the image, the fish was giving him an identical look.

"Don't act like you're so superior," he said to the fish with a roll of his eyes. "You're about to be dinner."

And Coop – how dare Coop look at him like he was wasting his life, like he was rotting away in this cabin, doing all the things he had never wanted for himself and pretending it made any difference to the fact that he had been too late to save Coop? How dare Coop look at him like he was selfish for not doing anything about the other chipped workers who had people they loved grieving for them?

He blinked at the turn of his thoughts. Coop kept on looking at him. So did the fish – as if *it* had any room to talk.

"Fine," he snapped to them both. "Fine. You win. I'll do it."

He knew what Coop would really have wanted from him.

He had known since he had first come here.

A knot in his shoulders that he had stopped noticing disappeared all at once, leaving him blinking at the sense of lightness, the sudden absence of pressure.

He turned his back on the fish and strode back out the door, pausing only to slip on his shoes.

Time to stop trying to be invisible, and start getting to know his neighbors a bit better. He already had a couple of ideas about which of them might have resistance contacts.

You win, Coop. You win.

ABOUT THE AUTHOR

A hermit at heart with a twisted mind, Lux Thorn is a lifelong whump enthusiast with a weakness for death scenes. They live in northern New England with their partner and child. They love swimming in the ocean, staying up late reading, and big floofy dogs.

BEFORE YOU GO

This is the ninth book in 12 Months of Whump, a series of whumpy novellas published by WPP throughout 2025. Each novella can be read as a standalone.

To stay up to date with the 12 Months of Whump series and other whumperfly-inducing projects, visit us at https://thewhumpyprintingpress.tumblr.com/